Fabulous Fathers

He didn't need this.

He didn't need to go chasing after a woman. No matter how great her legs were. No matter how provocative her mouth had been beneath his.

No question about it, though. Maggie McGuire was getting beneath Joe's skin. That wasn't good.

Worse, she'd been right in her assessment of his life. He did have a full plate. He had three adorable little girls to care for, provide for and raise. He certainly didn't need to get romantically involved with someone now. Especially someone who wasn't even receptive to the idea.

But if Maggie wasn't receptive to the idea of becoming involved with him, why had she kissed him like that?

Damn. Women should come with road maps.

Joe sighed. *And* a book of instructions.

Dear Reader,

This month, Silhouette Romance has a wonderful lineup—
sure to add love and laughter to your sunny summer days
and sultry nights. Marie Ferrarella starts us off with another
FABULOUS FATHER in *The Women in Joe Sullivan's Life*.
Sexy Joe Sullivan was an expert on *grown* women, but when
he suddenly finds himself raising three small nieces, he needs
the help of Maggie McGuire—and finds himself falling
for her womanly charms as well as her maternal instinct!
Cassandra Cavannaugh has plans for her own BUNDLE OF
JOY in Julianna Morris's *Baby Talk*. And Jake O'Connor
had no intention of being part of them. Can true love turn
Mr. Wrong into a perfect father—and husband for Cassie?

Dorsey Kelley spins another thrilling tale for WRANGLERS
AND LACE in *Cowboy for Hire*. Bent Murray thought
his rodeo days were behind him, until sassy cowgirl
Kate Monahan forced him to face his past—and her place
in his heart. Handsome Michael Damian gets more than
he bargained for in Christine Scott's *Imitation Bride*.
Lacey Keegan was only pretending to be his fiancée, but
now that wedding plans were snowballing, he began
wishing that their make-believe romance was real.

Two more stories with humor and love round out the
month in *Second Chance at Marriage* by Pamela Dalton,
and *An Improbable Wife* by debut author Sally Carleen.

Happy Reading!

Anne Canadeo

Senior Editor, Silhouette Romance

Please address questions and book requests to:
Silhouette Reader Service
U.S.: 3010 Walden Ave., P.O. Box 1325, Buffalo, NY 14269
Canadian: P.O. Box 609, Fort Erie, Ont. L2A 5X3

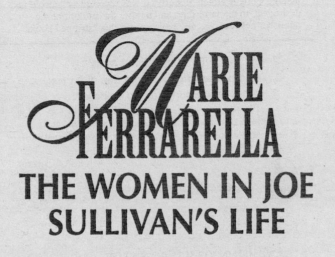

MARIE FERRARELLA

THE WOMEN IN JOE SULLIVAN'S LIFE

Silhouette

R O M A N C E™

Published by Silhouette Books

America's Publisher of Contemporary Romance

To Michael and Mark,
who never quite believed that older sisters
were supposed to be bossy.
Love,
Ma-ee-sha.

 SILHOUETTE BOOKS

ISBN 0-373-19096-4

THE WOMEN IN JOE SULLIVAN'S LIFE

Copyright © 1995 by Marie Rydzynski-Ferrarella

This edition published by arrangement with Harlequin Books S.A.

® and TM are trademarks of Harlequin Books S.A., used under license.
Trademarks indicated with ® are registered in the United States Patent
and Trademark Office, the Canadian Trade Marks Office and in other
countries.

Printed in U.S.A.

MARIE FERRARELLA

lives in Southern California. She describes herself as the tired mother of two overenergetic children and the contented wife of one wonderful man. She is thrilled to be following her dream of writing full-time.

Joe Sullivan on Fatherhood...

Boy, talk about instant fatherhood. One day I'm a bachelor with a simple life, with no bigger decision to make than what to have for dinner. The next day I'm responsible for three little girls, with a mountain of decisions to make. Daily. I can't say that it didn't shake me up. Or that I was equal to it. But the funny thing is that I *was* equal to it. Not right away. Not by myself. I had the love, but not the ability. That took a little redirection from someone with a great deal more experience with children than I had. Maggie McGuire began as the subject of an interview and turned into a godsend who helped me find my way through this confusing wonderland called fatherhood. I couldn't have made it without her.

Now, looking back, I realize that the simple life I had wasn't so much simple as it was empty. I know it's never going to be simple or empty again. And I couldn't be happier.

Chapter One

"You're not going to believe what's waiting in the reception area to talk to you."

Maggie McGuire raised her eyes from the financial report her brother had just handed her. The smile on her secretary's normally somber face was a mixture of bemusement and bewilderment.

"Girl Scouts selling cookies?" Maggie hazarded. It was the most outlandish thing she could think of, since this *was* the headquarters for both Magnificent Cookies' offices and plant.

"More like girls scouting for cookies." Ada's hazel eyes crinkled at the corners before her expression resumed its customary dour appearance.

Maggie hadn't the faintest idea what Ada was talking about. She exchanged looks with her brother. "Are you expecting anyone?"

Ethan shook his head. He had no appointments scheduled until early afternoon. In any event, anyone coming to see him would have been at his office, not Maggie's. "Not at the moment. You?"

Maggie was about to echo Ethan's denial, then stopped. Her stomach lurched slightly, the way it might have had she been standing in an elevator that had just dropped half a floor. She remembered. And frowned.

"Yes, I am." She sighed. "I promised to do an interview."

After twenty-six years, Ethan would have guessed that there weren't many things Maggie could have said that would have surprised him. This was one of them.

Two years separated them. Two years and an overwhelming wealth of responsibility. Maggie was the oldest. At age eleven, she had officially become a substitute mother to him and their two younger brothers, Adam and Richie. Eleven was when her mother, for years an alcoholic, had finally given up the will to live. Eleven was when Maggie had permanently surrendered her childhood.

It was Maggie who had held them together when their habitually unemployed father found his solace in an amber bottle. Maggie who made them feel safe as she promised that someday the trailer parks and thrift-shop clothes would all be a blurry memory. Maggie who swore that they'd never want again.

At times, Ethan thought with amusement, he believed that Maggie's name should have been Scarlett. It would have been fitting.

Maggie, in his eyes, was fearless, relentless and determined. She wasn't, however, a person who granted interviews. Even at his behest, when he thought it would help promote their quickly growing company and "really put them on the map," as Adam liked to say. Maggie, outwardly poised, charming and driven, was a very private person. No one knew it better than he did.

Maggie felt her brother's scrutiny. "What? You're looking at me as if I've just grown another head."

"No, I'm looking at you as if I don't know you," Ethan clarified. He gathered the sheets of the report together. It had been a banner quarter, following on the heels of several others like it. Maggie had lived up to her promise, but then, he had always believed that she would. "An interview? You?"

It pleased her that she could still surprise him after all these years. God knew her moment of weakness had surprised her. "An interview. Me."

He tucked the sheets into a crimson folder. "Not that I think it's a bad thing. It's a good thing." He wondered what had caused her to come around to his way of thinking. Maggie tended to forge her own path without consulting anyone until after the fact. At times it made him feel a little frustrated. Not to mention useless. "I've always said that," he reminded her. "But what made you change your mind?"

She lifted her shoulders and let them drop as she rose. "The editor who called promised it was going to be a short piece. Adam kept nagging how publicity—the warm touch—could only help. So I said yes." *In a moment when I should have had my head examined.* "It'll be a good precursor for the commercial that I—" her eyes slid toward Ethan "—that *we* are going to shoot."

Maggie's slip made him smile. She was trying, he thought. No one could deny that. After years of doing everything on her own, he fully appreciated the fact that it was hard for his sister to relinquish even a shred of control. She was too accustomed to overseeing every last detail. It was going to make her old before her time if she wasn't careful. Not to mention driving the rest of them up a wall.

Ada huffed and cleared her throat loudly, bringing the focus back to her problem, which in her opinion neither of them seemed to understand.

"Look, before the reception area—" she spread-eagled a spidery hand across her shallow chest "—*my* area, becomes a shambles, can I bring them in here?"

Maybe it wasn't the free-lance writer, after all. Maggie glanced down at her calendar and saw the time she had hastily scribbled down. The man was already late. Maybe he wasn't coming.

A touch of relief slivered down her spine and her stomach unknotted. "Them?"

Ada's head bobbed once. "Them." All traces of humor gone now, she said the single word as if she were announcing the advent of a plague.

Ada was a wonder as a secretary, but she tended to be overdramatic. Amusement had Maggie relaxing a little more. "Wasn't there a science-fiction movie by that name? About giant ants?" Maggie glanced at her brother for confirmation. He merely shrugged.

"Close enough," Ada assured her. She glanced over her shoulder at the closed door as if she could somehow divine what was going on beyond it.

Ethan circumvented the older woman and reached for the doorknob. He glanced at Maggie. "I don't know about you, but she's got me curious."

Whatever Ethan thought he was prepared for when he opened the door, it wasn't what he saw. There was a handsome, slightly beleaguered blond-haired man standing beside Ada's desk. He was surrounded by three very animated little girls, also blond. The oldest didn't look to be any older than eight.

Maggie nudged Ethan aside. Her brother was a full foot taller than she was and it made visibility difficult. When she saw the girls, her curiosity instantly turned to amusement. Adam obviously had failed to tell the casting office that calls for the cookie commercial weren't going out until the end of the week. Trust Adam to forget little details like that. His head was always in the clouds.

Her eyes shifted from the girls to the man with them. He seemed to be having a great deal of difficulty restraining their exuberance.

This was a twist, she thought. A stage father instead of a stage mother.

Maggie was smiling as she stepped forward. Her eyes were on the man. "I'm sorry. There's been some misunderstanding. You're not supposed to be here until next week." The little girls made her think of unharnessed, pure energy. This had to be their first commercial. They were rather adorable, she thought. "And then by appointment only."

Joe Sullivan turned to look at the woman who spoke, his free hand firmly wrapped around his youngest niece's. There was a potted ficus tree by the elevator that Jennifer had been eyeing much too intently. He could see it denuded of its leaves in five minutes flat. Of his three nieces, four-year-old Jennifer was the fastest. Also the most destructive.

"But I've *got* an appointment."

He probably did, Maggie thought. Another oversight. She really had to find the time to talk to Adam about writing things down. Maggie glanced at Ethan over her shoulder. "Tell Adam that when he makes appointments for me, he should tell me."

"Mr. McGuire didn't make an appointment with him."

Maggie looked at Ada in surprise.

The secretary nodded at the man whose name she'd just taken. "You did. With his editor. The interview?" she prompted when the light still failed to enter Maggie's eyes. "Remember?"

Maggie looked at the tall man before her. Damn. "You're with *County Magazine*?"

If he didn't know any better, Joe Sullivan would have sworn that the very classy-looking woman before him looked just a touch horrified. But why would anyone be horrified of *County Magazine*? It wasn't as if *County Magazine* was a supermarket tabloid. It was a widely read, respected magazine that basically had a good word to say about everything.

"Yes, I am."

Butterflies suddenly erupted in Maggie's stomach and began fluttering. Butterflies that were a holdover from the past. They belonged to Maggie McGuire, the girl in hand-me-downs and thrift-shop shoes, not Southern California's Businesswoman of the Year. There was no use trying to calm them. Maggie had come to terms with the fact that she could never leave that young girl far behind. She was very much a part of everything she did. Maybe even the *cause* of everything she did.

Maggie looked at the little girls again. They looked as if they were dying to break free. One of them was eyeing Ada's computer as if it were the latest toy on the market. If this man was with *County Magazine,* what was he doing with these children? Why had he brought them with him?

She shook her head. "I'm afraid that I don't understand."

There was, Joe knew, a great deal to understand. He only hoped that Maggie McGuire's disposition was half as sweet as the ingredients in her chocolate chip cookie, which had taken Southern California, and subsequently the West, by storm.

At times he still didn't understand any of it himself. God knew he hadn't been able to make any sense of the tragedy that had suddenly robbed three small girls of their parents and turned him from a carefree bachelor into a bachelor father.

For the last two long, harrowing months, as he had attempted to come to terms with his own grief, Joseph Sullivan had also been struggling to restructure his admittedly chaotic life to make a place and a home for his three young nieces, Sandy, Christine and Jennifer.

Whole libraries, he had decided very early in this endeavor, could have been filled with what he didn't know about parenting. It seemed as if every minute brought with it a new decision to make. Or a fresh new squabble to referee.

He had fervently hoped that the lack of his knowledge could have been supplemented by the woman he had quickly hired to care for the girls. The same woman who had abruptly quit this morning without notice after he had up-braided her for making seven-year-old Sandy cry.

Panic had hit him as he watched the formidable woman walk down his driveway toward the waiting taxi, suitcase in hand. He had an interview to conduct in an hour. An inter-view that did *not* call for three nieces to tag along.

The interview with Maggie McGuire, president of Mag-nificent Cookies, was an important one. His editor had made it clear that it couldn't be rescheduled when he had called him with his dilemma. His back to the wall, Joe had then called everyone he knew. Those who weren't at their jobs had apparently disappeared off the face of the earth, leaving Joe with three nieces and no options.

After resorting to cajoling and bribery, he'd packed all three into the car and driven to the industrial complex that housed the newly relocated Magnificent Cookies head-quarters and plant.

Miracles, he'd heard, happened all the time. All he needed was a tiny one. He needed the girls to behave for an hour. Joe figured that came under the heading of a miracle if anything did, "I know this doesn't look very orthodox, and I'm sorry I'm late, but I am here to do the interview."

Maggie observed the little girls. For the moment, they *were* standing still. But hard-earned experience told her that she was in the presence of ticking bombs waiting to be det-onated.

Some of her butterflies abated in the face of this added twist and the man's visible discomfort. This might not be so bad after all. Maggie turned toward her brother and she nodded at the folder he was holding.

"We'll talk some more later about the projections you're making."

Ethan nodded, almost reluctant to leave. He had a feeling this was going to get more interesting. "Have fun," he quipped as he went down the hall.

From the look on Ada's face, Maggie guessed that the woman was ready to sweep the lot of them toward the exit. Ada had apparently seen the middle one eyeing her computer.

"Then you are Mr. Sullivan?" Maggie asked for form's sake. She vaguely remembered the editor mentioning the man's name when he'd made the arrangements with her.

With one hand holding his briefcase and one attached to Jennifer, Joe had none to offer Maggie. So he nodded instead. "Yes. But it's Joe, please."

He watched in dismay as Sandy and Christine ducked into Maggie's office. He didn't like not being in control of a situation, and this was as far from control as he'd ever been. He flashed Maggie an apologetic smile. "Maybe we had better postpone your interview." He hoped that, after seeing his problem, she would change her mind about rescheduling.

Maggie shook her head. If she rescheduled, that only meant she'd have more time to think about this. More time to dread it. She didn't like talking about herself. The editor had gotten her in a weak moment. Since she was committed, she wanted to get this over with. Now.

"No, that's all right. I don't mind a little chaos," she murmured. *Or a lot.*

She gestured toward her office. It was a little after the fact, she noted wryly, since two of the girls had already taken it upon themselves to dart in. The girl tethered to Sullivan was yanking him in for all she was worth. All three looked like tiny replicas of him. She assumed they were his daughters.

Joe placed his briefcase down on the first available space, the small coffee table, and caught Christine by the hand. Alone, Sandy settled down at his side, content to be the only free one of her siblings.

Bribery, he realized sadly, didn't go nearly as far as he'd hoped. On the way over he'd promised the girls that they would stop at their favorite toy store after the interview, but only if they were on their best behavior this afternoon. Obviously their ''best'' fell way below his expectations.

There was a time he wouldn't have minded. As their uncle, he had doted on the girls, seeing them whenever the opportunity arose. Visits were short and the main ingredient had always been fun.

Bringing them along on an interview put a completely different light on the situation. Parenting had placed another dimension on their relationship, one he felt ill-equipped to handle. It was totally foreign to him. The only discipline he'd ever applied was to himself, and that was lax at best. He didn't know what to do where the girls were concerned.

But if he didn't find a way to make them behave, and soon, he was going to be in big trouble. Starting now, he imagined.

The last thing Maggie saw as she closed the door was the reproving expression on Ada's face. Maggie turned to face the small group gathered in her office. The girls looked as if they were twitching to get loose.

''If you don't mind my asking, did you bring along your own food tasters?''

Chagrined, Joe dropped Jennifer's hand and dragged his fingers through his hair. Freed, Jennifer took the opportunity to climb up on the cream leather sofa that was against the wall. The buckles on her shoes threatened to permanently scar the material.

With a frustrated sigh that Maggie found more amusing than annoying, Joe scooped the little girl up from the sofa. He had to let go of the other little girl in order to do so.

He looked about as helpless as a man could, Maggie thought.

Joe set Jennifer down. ''It's just that I couldn't get a sitter—''

Where was his wife, Maggie wondered. Probably running for the hills, not that she could blame her. Although the girls were adorable, she'd been this route herself and knew how devastatingly tiring it could be.

Still, amusement at his dilemma curved the corners of her mouth. "I think I'd say, in all fairness, that you'd probably need more than one."

He gave her a sheepish look as he glanced over his shoulder. He had just coaxed Christine away from the beige-coloured blinds. Joe thought of the girls' former nanny, the very tight-lipped Mrs. Garrick. The girls had proved to be more than her match. "You're right on that score."

The girls were very obviously sisters. And just as obviously related to him. Still, she could be wrong. "I take it they're all yours."

The girls stopped, as if frozen on videotape, and looked at him. Joe tried to sound as reassuring as possible. "As of two months ago."

Maggie raised a brow as she surveyed the girls. That was an odd way to put it. "I think in this case you might be the more interesting interview."

He laughed, relieved that she wasn't annoyed. As unorthodox as this was, maybe it still had a prayer of working out.

It wasn't as if his entire future depended on this article, but the series on the five most prominent businesswomen in Orange County had been his brainchild and he had written all the other installments. Though he was laid back in all other aspects of his life, his work was very important to him. Doing a credible job was just as important to him. And interviewing the heretofore rather elusive Maggie McGuire would be a nice finish to the series.

His laughter seemed to waft all around her. Instantly, Maggie found herself literally enveloped by the warm, rich sound. It wound through her like a hot, seductive first cup of coffee on a brisk, cold morning, making her feel peaceful, and yet, oddly enough, just the slightest bit stirred, as well. Not on edge, just alerted.

As if something was coming.

It was a silly notion and she shook it off. That was what she got for putting in sixteen-hour days. Hallucinations about a man's laugh.

Joe nodded toward his nieces. Sandy stood beside him, but Christine had once again abandoned her post, intent on exploring an overflowing bookcase. As calmly as possible, Joe made a grab for the edge of Christine's dress. Catching it, he anchored the girl in place.

Christine squirmed, then, as if resigned to a momentary lull in the game, stood still.

Joe knew it wasn't for long, but he would take whatever he could get. The danger momentarily at bay, Joe's attention refocused on Maggie. "I'm glad you have a sense of humor."

"I'm equally glad you have quick hands." She nodded toward the niece he had tethered. Joe grinned at her response. Something in his gaze, warm and sensual, washed over her.

She dismissed it. Maggie lowered her eyes to her desk and pressed the speaker phone. If they were going to get on with this, she was going to need a diversion for the girls.

"Ada, would you bring in a tray of cookies, please?" She saw the girls' eyes light up with anticipation. Maggie smiled. Music might not soothe the savage beasts, but she knew through experience that cookies would. At least temporarily. "As you so astutely noted earlier, I think I might have some customers for us."

Straightening, Maggie crossed to the trio. She could remember, without too much effort, when her brothers were that age, a rambunctious handful who seemed to fill every available speck of space within the endless succession of rundown trailer homes they'd lived in. Though she hated that confinement and the overwhelming burden she'd had to shoulder in those days, something suspiciously like nostalgia whispered faintly in the back corners of her mind.

For the moment, Joe had them lined up before the sofa, three little dolls whose batteries were about to kick in. Maggie inclined her head as she looked at them. "Hi, I'm Maggie."

Joe noted with surprise that there wasn't a hint of cloying condescension in her voice.

The most competitive, Christine responded first. "I'm Christine." She pointed to herself, then vaguely waved the same finger toward her sisters, far more nonchalantly. "That's Sandy and Jennifer. Sandy's older, but I'm better," she concluded importantly, certain this was the only piece of information that mattered.

Maggie's eyes shifted toward Sandy. She remembered herself at that age. The same insecurities that had plagued her appeared to be in the little girl's blue eyes. Maggie felt a wisp of kinship stirring.

"Being the oldest is rough," she confided to Sandy. "Isn't it?"

Sandy looked surprised at being singled out while Christine was talking. The latter pouted, her small hands making fists at her waist. Sandy nodded, her straight blond hair bobbing up and down. Her eyes shifted toward her sisters before coming to rest on the tops of her scuffed black shoes.

"Yeah."

Maggie heard a great deal in that single word. Or maybe, she thought, she was just reading her own past into it.

"And you never really outgrow it," Maggie murmured under her breath.

She raised her eyes. Sullivan was studying her very carefully. She was going to have to watch that, she thought. The man was a journalist and capable of making an issue out of a passing, unguarded moment.

His scrutiny made her uncomfortable. It was all part of the interview, of course, and expected. But she felt vaguely unsettled by it, though she was fairly certain that she didn't show it. Over the years, she had gotten quite adept at keeping the outside world away from her inner thoughts. Her inner fears. Fearful people didn't succeed in this world. Her father had proven that to her over and over again.

She had no intentions of ending up like her father. Or her mother, either. Maggie Fiona McGuire had no intentions of ever letting down anyone who depended on her, the way both her parents had.

Maggie drew a breath as she turned her attention toward Sullivan. "As for my sense of humor, Mr. Sullivan," she continued smoothly, "I wouldn't be caught dead without it."

And from the looks of it, she mused as the girls began to squirm again, she was definitely going to need it for the next half hour or so.

Joe realized that he was staring at her again. He hadn't meant to. This interview was already as unorthodox as anyone could have been asked to tolerate. He didn't want to push his luck any further by staring at the woman like some adolescent with a bad case of hormonal flare-up.

Not that she wasn't something to look at. Maggie McGuire was a great deal more attractive in person than that eight-by-ten glossy that the research department had sent to him had led him to believe.

There was no way that a flat, two-dimensional photograph could have begun to capture the sheer vitality that seemed to exude from the woman. He'd done his background digging well and knew that she was the sole driving power behind the company, a hands-on president who'd been deservedly honored by her peers. From her auburn hair to her brilliant green eyes, she was pure energy. There was an aura around her, an invisible glow that was just shy of being tangible. It made a man sit up and take notice.

And just possibly, he thought, beg.

Chapter Two

Before Joe could begin his interview, Maggie's secretary entered the office. She was carrying a large black lacquered tray. The surface was almost completely covered with neat piles of large chocolate chip cookies.

The sight scarcely had time to register before he heard the squeal of anticipation rising up around him. But, to his utter amazement, Sandy, Christine and Jennifer didn't descend upon the tray's contents like a ravenous horde when it was set down on the coffee table. They seemed to be actually waiting for permission.

Maybe his little pep talk on the way over had finally set in and done some good, after all.

Sandy's eyes were as huge as the cookies on the tray. "Are these for us?" The question was directed to Maggie rather than her uncle.

She obviously sensed who was in charge here, Joe thought. He glanced toward Maggie and wondered if she was one of those people who always needed to be in control of things. For his part, he didn't need to control anything but his own destiny. That, unfortunately, was completely out of control for the moment. But he was working on it, working on turning the girls and him into a true family.

Maggie noted that Ada withdrew from the room with a very dubious expression on her face. Ada was single and had trouble relating to anything under three feet that didn't have fur on it.

Turning toward the girls, Maggie focused her attention on the three eager sets of hands that were all but twitching at the girls' sides. "Yes, these are for you. I hope you enjoy them."

She might as well have said, "Let the eating begin." It was as if a gun had gone off, signaling the start of a feeding frenzy. Hands shot out at the mountain of cookies from all directions. The girls were apparently determined to whittle it down to size in record time.

If they were eating, Joe reasoned, they couldn't cause any damage. To insure the fact that he would have at least a small space of time in which to conduct the interview, he took out the coloring books and crayons that he'd thought to bring with him from his briefcase. He placed them on the sofa next to Sandy and stepped back.

None of the girls noticed the coloring books.

"I think that should keep them busy for a while." He observed his nieces for a moment longer, just to make sure that he wasn't living in a fool's paradise.

The three girls, each having staked out a different portion of the tray, were propped up on their knees, gleefully chewing away and giggling. It was nice to see them this way, he thought. There'd been a while there when he hadn't been sure if they could shake off the oppressive wraps of sorrow. But they had. Except for Sandy.

Joe looked at Maggie and grinned. "I guess I'm lucky that you make cookies and not computer chips."

There was something a little bit too stimulating about his grin, Maggie thought. She shifted her eyes toward the girls.

"In that case, I would have found computer games for them to play with."

He had been right. She was clearly a lady who was not overwhelmed by any situation she found herself in. It was an admirable quality. And in her, a rather sexy one.

"An answer for everything." His eyes swept over her. "Pretty resilient, aren't you?"

Maggie looked at him sharply and decided that he wasn't playing up to her. A lot of people did these days. She never trusted flattery. It was usually self-serving and empty. And sometimes dangerous if taken to heart. "It's an attribute I try to cultivate."

No doubt. Joe nodded as he picked up a cookie. He bit into it absently, eager to get on with the interview. There was no telling how long this lull with the girls would last.

Flavor seemed to explode in his mouth. He looked at the remainder of the cookie in his hand as if it had just whispered a secret to him.

"Not bad." He motioned with the cookie.

"Not bad?" Maggie echoed. An amused smile lifted the corners of her mouth. Obviously no one had trained this man in the art of being obsequious. "Aren't you supposed to flatter me a little more, or is 'not bad' considered high praise coming from you?"

Very deliberately, Joe took another bite out of the cookie. His eyes never left hers. Something fluttered in her stomach. She ignored it, telling herself that it was the interview that was making her uneasy.

Joe made himself comfortable on the chair in front of Maggie's desk. Crossing one leg over his thigh, he thoughtfully studied the remainder of the cookie in his hand.

"Actually, this has to be the 'chocolatiest' chocolate chip cookie I have ever had." He nibbled on it again, letting the crumbs melt on his tongue the way a wine taster might sample a brand-new wine. "And there's something more?—" He looked at her, silently asking Maggie if he was right.

Maggie smiled, pleased that he'd detected a difference. A lot of people just wolfed the cookies down, never fully realizing why they preferred hers over another brand. Though the sales still added up, aesthetically it wasn't enough for her. Maggie wanted people to consciously note the difference.

"Yes."

He eyed the last piece for a moment before setting it aside on the desk. He hadn't come to eat, but to work. "What is it?"

Did he actually think she was going to blurt it out so that he could write the recipe up for everyone to read? He was either very naive, or thought she was.

"That's not for public knowledge." Her eyes sparkled as she told him. She looked, he thought, like a young girl who was privy to an exclusive, precious secret and felt special because of it. "It's what separates us from the mass-market cookies."

It was probably just a dash of one thing or another, he mused. Still, the taste lingered on his tongue, much like a sweet kiss. He raised his eyes to her lips before continuing. "Did you pay someone to develop it for you?"

For just the briefest of moments, when he had looked up at her, she'd felt a warm flash over her. The next instant, she blinked and it was gone.

Maggie shook her head. "No, I developed it." The surprised look on his face pleased her unexpectedly. "One rainy day when I ran out of sugar," she added, then stopped. There was no sense in giving him too many details. They might trip her up. He didn't need to know that she had gotten her brothers involved in baking cookies as a way of keeping them all together when they had been very young. There'd been no television set for them to watch, no money to spend on movies. So she had baked, and spun stories as she did so, filling their heads and their stomachs at the same time.

He twirled what was left of the cookie between his thumb and forefinger. Joe raised his eyes to hers. "And there's no chance?—"

Her eyes laughed at him. "Not even remotely."

"Didn't think so."

But there was no harm in asking. He wondered if a lab could analyze a sample and if it would be worth the trouble. There were a lot of cookie companies out there. And enough stomachs to go around.

Suddenly realizing that it was awfully quiet, Joe glanced over his shoulder. The girls were still circled around the tray, systematically working their way down. All except for Jennifer, who was nibbling away at the perimeter. She had a cookie in each hand and what appeared to be the remainder of one stuffed in her mouth. Weighing in at a little more than thirty-eight pounds, his youngest niece was less of a little girl than a methodical eating machine. She took after his brother, he thought with a pang. Alec used to eat as if he could never get his fill and had remained thin all his life.

He banished the jagged memory and concentrated on what he had to do. Sitting back, Joe looked at Maggie again. "Well, thanks to those cookies and their secret ingredient, I think we'll be able to manage this in peace and quiet. Are you ready to begin the interview?"

It was meant as a rhetorical question. He hadn't expected anything but a nod from her.

Maggie pressed her lips together as she watched the girls. "May I ask you a question first?"

He wondered what was on her mind. "I guess that's only fair, seeing as how I invaded your territory."

Standing near him, she leaned a hip against her desk and nodded toward the girls. "Do you usually bring them along with you on interviews?"

He knew he owed her an explanation, especially since she was being so nice about it.

"No, this is a first, unfortunately. Like I said, I really couldn't get a sitter. And their nanny decided that today was a good day to quit." He glanced toward the girls and re-membered how Sandy had cried. It had been difficult containing his anger against the sharp-tongued woman. "I guess it was good for all of us." Maggie was looking at him curiously. "They're my nieces." He decided not to go any further with the explanation than that.

Rummaging through his briefcase, he took out a pad. His tape recorder was nestled next to it. He left it there. Instinctively, he sensed that she wasn't the type who liked having a machine take down her every word.

"Then they're not your children?" The way he had phrased things earlier had made her think that perhaps he and the girls' mother were divorced and he had been awarded custody.

He raised his eyes to hers. "They are now. My brother and sister-in-law were killed two months ago in a car accident."

"Oh." For a moment, the very air had left her lungs. It always did when she thought of death. Anyone's death. It reminded her of the morning she had found her mother. Too many pills had mingled with Fiona McGuire's usual consumption of whiskey. Maggie had known in that instant that she was staring at someone whom death had claimed. She had ushered the boys off to school and then called the police. Her father didn't come home for two days. "I'm very sorry."

She was, he thought. He had no idea why, but she was. "Yeah," he said slowly. "So am I. This is all so new to me, sometimes I'm afraid I'm really messing things up for them."

The girls looked none the worse for wear. "Children are pretty resilient." Memories nudged one another, slipping through her mind, bold and vivid and unannounced. "You'll find that when necessary, children can raise themselves."

There was a faraway note in her voice that made him think she was speaking from experience. It was time to turn the interview away from him and toward her.

"Did you?"

The quietly probing question caught her off guard. She had let too much slip. Curving her lips into a wide smile, she shook her head. "I'm just quoting from a child psychology course I once took."

Clearing her throat, she straightened and retreated behind her desk. She felt better having some distance between them.

Poised, ready, Maggie smiled at Joe and took her seat. "Now then, I believe that you'd like to ask me some questions."

Joe had the distinct feeling he'd just entered a press meeting rather than a one-on-one interview.

A lot of questions, he thought, taking out his pen. *And some of them would be off the record.*

Forty-five minutes later, Joe Sullivan felt as if he had just been led through a very subtly orchestrated bout of shadow boxing.

Maggie McGuire had told him everything he wanted to know about the company she had begun in her kitchen a little more than five years ago. In the same easy, gregarious manner, she had evaded every single question he'd asked her about herself except for the most impersonal of details. He'd learned that she graduated from the University of California at Irvine with a business degree, having put herself through school at night. He also learned that she strongly believed in nepotism and utilized it when hiring people for her company.

When he questioned her about it, she smiled broadly and the tiny line of tension he'd noticed in her jaw disappeared. It was the first unguarded moment Joe had observed during the interview.

"If you employ family members and friends, Mr. Sulllvan, you have people working for you who feel as if they have more than just a cursory interest in the business. They're building something with you."

Studying her, he decided that she really believed what she was saying. He played devil's advocate. "And just what do they get out of all this effort, besides their paychecks?"

"Pride. And a share of the profits. A share in the company they're building." Maggie was quite adamant about that. Everyone who worked at Magnificent Cookies owned a piece of it.

She leaned back, in her element now. Maggie made it a point to know everyone who worked for her. The company was still small enough for that. She hoped it always would be. "I believe in fostering a sense of family togetherness here."

She wasn't just mouthing platitudes that would look good in print; she was serious, he thought. Maybe that was the secret to the company's rather astronomical rise from nothing to a contender in less than five years. Maybe she was on to something at that. He glanced at the cookie he'd set aside when he began writing.

"The cookie with a heart." Joe looked at her with a grin. "Not bad for a slogan." It was time to hone in on the true focus of his series. He indicated his notes. "I'm going to need more background."

Ada had brought her several of their promotional pamphlets that Maggie customarily used in her marketing blitzes. She and Ethan had personally flown to meet with the presidents of several supermarket chains and talked their way onto the markets' shelves, leaving a flattering paper trail in their wake.

Maggie indicated the pamphlets, pushing them toward Joe. "It's all in there."

Joe dutifully collected the pamphlets and deposited the literature into his briefcase. "Thanks, but the background I was interested in was yours."

Their eyes held for a moment as something seemed to crackle between them. Maggie forced a smile to her lips as she spread her hands. "What you see is what you get, Mr. Sullivan."

He sincerely doubted it. She was being elusive. It was becoming very obvious that he wasn't going to get any more information out of her on that score. Yet.

Joe knew there had to be more. There always was. He felt his interest being aroused. Just what was her story? Who was she? What motivated her? These were questions he knew the readers wanted answered.

And so did he.

He leaned forward in his chair, his eyes on her face. "Yes, but what exactly do I see?"

His question, though delivered with humor, was far too personal for her liking. This kind of probing was one of the reasons she had discouraged past interviews. She didn't like the idea of being exposed to satisfy the public's curiosity.

Or anyone else's, she added silently, looking at Joe. Though she was outgoing, underneath it all she was a private person with private hurts she wasn't about to uncover.

What mattered was the integrity of the product she sold, nothing else.

"What you see is a successful businesswoman," she replied.

Maggie slid her fingers idly along the small statuette that stood on the corner of her desk, the one she'd been given by the League of Southern California Businesswomen. She would have been lying if she had said that it hadn't been a thrill to win it. Receiving the recognition had validated her and the struggle she'd gone through. It validated the energy she'd devoted to making something of herself and bringing her family along with her.

But it wasn't the end of the line. She doubted that there ever would be an end of the line for her. There was always one more hill to climb, one more mile to place between herself and the specter of poverty she never seemed to be able to escape.

Though she appeared cool and in control, Joe felt as if he'd somehow struck a nerve. He just didn't know which one and why.

"All right, and what made you that way?"

He didn't give up. Tenacity was a quality she'd nurtured in herself and encouraged in her brothers. It made her just a wee bit nervous in someone else.

"Drive."

Not good enough, he thought. This wasn't going to be the easy puff piece he'd envisioned when he'd originally pitched it to his editor. He did his best work when challenged. Joe dug in. "Why?"

Maggie unconsciously raised her chin, defensive. "Why not?"

She wasn't about to give an inch, he thought. Why? What was she hiding so zealously?

"This is an interview, Ms. McGuire, not a free association test." He indicated his notes. They could be transcribed into an enjoyable article, but as it stood, what he had down was hardly penetrating. It offered less than a glimpse into the soul of the woman who'd accomplished a great deal in a very short time. The fact that she didn't allow that glimpse, he thought, was rather telling. There was a real story here. "I want something a little meatier than this."

Maggie felt as if she were being hemmed in and she didn't care for it. She rose abruptly. She was still pleasant, but a great deal of distance had suddenly erupted between them. "I can take you on a tour of the plant."

Joe gained his feet just as she moved past his chair, uncoiling more than actually rising. The very movement seemed to challenge her. Instinctively, Maggie took a step back, though she didn't lower her eyes.

The lady had a hell of a lot more than just cookies and secret recipes going for her. "That would be very nice, but

I'm not doing a story on how cookies are made. I'm doing a story on how a successful businesswoman is made—"

His manner wasn't threatening so much as relentless. But she was more than a match for it. And she'd given him as much as she intended to.

"Then I'm afraid—"

Maggie's words were cut off by a heartwrenching, pitiful moan. She and Joe turned to look at the girls, whom they had all but forgotten in the last few minutes. Jennifer moaned loudly again, clutching her stomach, as her sisters gathered around her.

Christine looked fascinated and repulsed at the same time. "Uncle Joe, Jenny's sick." Her mouth became a perfect O as she looked at her younger sister, and then she squealed. "She's going to—"

There was no need for Christine to finish her high-pitched announcement. It was abundantly clear to everyone what Jenny was about to do.

The next moment, she did it.

Startled, concerned, embarrassed and numbed, Joe watched in horror as his four-year-old niece proceeded to swiftly recycle the cookies she had been polishing off with such abandonment and aplomb.

Joe felt as if his feet were glued to the rug. He was at a loss as to what to do first, other than to issue a heartfelt apology to the woman whose furnishings were being rechristened.

"Oh, Ms. McGuire, I'm sorry. I—" Joe didn't know whether to snatch Jennifer up and hold her, or begin cleaning the rug and coffee table. Or both. He'd never been within six feet of a sick child before without someone present who knew what he or she was doing.

Maggie hardly heard his apology. Her attention and her empathy was completely centered on Jennifer. Maggie had spent her share of evenings sitting beside a sick brother, holding his head and offering comfort as well as a bucket to retch in when the time called for it.

Wasting no time in answering Joe's apology, Maggie quickly grabbed her empty wastepaper basket and positioned it in front of the little girl. On her knees, unmindful of the small, messy streak along the hem of Jennifer's dress, Maggie held the child as Jennifer coughed and finished emptying out her stomach.

"Better?" Maggie asked.

Hiccuping, crying, Jennifer looked up at Maggie. Her eyes were bewildered and frightened.

"I guess not," Maggie murmured softly.

Pulling out a fistful of tissues from the dispenser on the coffee table, Maggie slowly cleaned the little girl's mouth. As she worked, she murmured soothing words to Jennifer.

Only partially aware of the fact that Sandy and Christine had clustered around him for moral support, Joe watched Maggie. Her kindly competence made him feel helpless, relieved and impressed all at the same time. Above all, he was grateful that she was here to handle this.

He bent down to Jennifer's level to attempt to reassure her. Jennifer hardly looked at him. His youngest niece was clutching Maggie as if Maggie was her only road to salvation.

"You have children of your own?" Joe addressed the question to the back of Maggie's head. He hadn't even found out that much, he realized. She had been very cagey in this interview.

Maggie offered Jennifer an encouraging smile. There was pure misery in the girl's blue eyes. That would be gone within the hour, Maggie judged.

"I raised my brothers," she answered mechanically, without thinking. She looked at him sharply. "I mean I helped raise them." Jennifer whimpered. "It's going to be all right, honey." Maggie smoothed Jennifer's hair away from her face. "You weren't supposed to try to eat a pile of cookies that are taller than you all by yourself. That's the secret." She winked.

Jennifer absorbed the words as gospel. The corners of her mouth drooped as she looked up at Maggie. "I don't feel so good."

Maggie successfully swallowed her laugh. "No, I don't imagine that you do." She felt Jennifer's forehead. It was cool. Nothing more than a severely upset stomach here, she decided. Guilt nudged her. She should have paid some attention to the girls. If she had, this wouldn't have happened. Her fault for letting her nerves get the better of her.

She looked over Jennifer's head at Sandy. "Sandy, would you please tell the lady outside my office that I need some soda pop sent in and quickly."

Eager to please, Sandy streaked out of the room.

Rising, Maggie picked Jennifer up. Carrying her easily on one hip, the way she once had Richie, Maggie crossed to the newly paneled wall on the far side of the office. As she lightly touched a space just at eye level, an entire floor-to-ceiling panel sprang open. Just inside was a small bathroom decorated in shell pink. This was the one luxury she allowed herself, in memory of all the times the six of them had had to share one tiny bathroom. To Maggie the bathroom was a sign that she had arrived.

If Christine's eyes had opened any wider, they would have fallen out, Joe thought, following in Maggie's wake.

Christine stood on the threshold of the bathroom, peering in hesitantly. "Is that like Aladdin's cave?"

Maggie laughed. "Only when Aladdin had to go to the bathroom."

Very gently, she set Jennifer down on the pink-tiled counter and turned on the faucet. The little girl was pumping her legs back and forth nervously as she watched Maggie. "Let's wash your face, okay?"

Pleased to be consulted, Jennifer nodded solemnly. "Okay."

With gentle strokes, Maggie washed away the telltale signs of recent distress from the girl's mouth. She was aware of the fact that Joe was silently watching her every movement, and it made her self-conscious. Maggie shut out the sensation and concentrated on the little girl.

"Lucky most of that yucky stuff hit the floor and not this pretty dress." Maggie shut off the faucet and smoothed the light yellow skirt. "Did you pick this out yourself?"

Jennifer nodded. "Uh-huh."

It was becoming apparent to Joe that Christine lived to contradict. "No, she didn't." Christine jerked a thumb at him. "Uncle Joe did."

Maggie saw the look of distress mounting again in Jennifer's face and was quick to smooth out the storm clouds. "Well, Uncle Joe has good taste."

Christine cocked her head, frowning as she tried to understand. "He didn't eat it, he picked it."

This one was going to be a lawyer, Maggie thought. If her sisters didn't kill her first.

"My mistake." Maggie picked Jennifer up and walked back into her office. Christine shadowed her steps.

"Soda's here," Sandy announced loudly, running in front of Ada.

Holding a can she'd gotten from the vending machine down the hall, Ada stopped short of the center of disaster. Her eyes were as wide as any of the children's had been. "Maggie, what's all that?—"

Maggie waved a dismissive hand, cutting Ada short. She didn't want to embarrass Jennifer any more than she assumed the little girl already was. "Call Maintenance for me and ask Pete to come up, will you? We've had a little accident."

"That's for sure." Ada backed up, though she was nowhere near the actual target area. She looked at the child in Maggie's arms. Maggie looked natural that way, Ada thought. Decorum indicated that she ask. "Do you need any help?"

Joe expected Maggie to readily surrender the situation to an underling. Anticipating her, he stepped forward to claim his niece. But Maggie surprised him by shaking her head.

Jennifer remained in her arms as Maggie took the soda can from Ada.

"No, everything's under control here." Maggie sat down and placed Jennifer on her lap, then popped the top on the can. She offered it to Jennifer. "Just sip a little of this, sweetie, and your tummy'll feel better soon." Knowing how much a child needed the assurance of an all-knowing adult, she added, "I promise."

Grasping the can with both hands, Jennifer did as she was told. Her eyes never left Maggie's face. Maggie smiled and smoothed the tangled hair away from the girl's face again.

To the best of his recollection, Joe couldn't remember ever seeing Jennifer this subdued except when she was fast asleep. He felt himself growing steadily more intrigued by the woman sitting on the sofa.

"Better?" Maggie asked again, hoping for a positive answer this time.

Jennifer raised her head. A drop of soda dribbled down her chin. She managed a crack of a smile. "Better."

Maggie looked over Jennifer's head at Joe. "I'd take her home if I were you. Nothing but clear liquids for the rest of the day. Then some crackers tonight."

Joe took his niece into his arms. He felt her reluctance to leave Maggie. Under similar circumstances, he would be reluctant, too, he mused.

The corner of his mouth quirked as he took in her advice. "And chicken soup?"

In her opinion, chicken soup was highly underrated. "Not a bad idea." Maggie rose and dusted off her skirt. It was going to need a trip to the cleaners. "Don't feed her anything you can't see through." She ticked things off on her fingers from long experience. "No juices except for apple. Give her gelatin tonight." She glanced at the tray Ada had set down on the coffee table less than an hour ago. "And no cookies."

"Awwww." The mournful cry rose from the other two girls.

She saw the slightly haggard look entering Joe's eyes. "I tell you what. My secretary will give you each a big bag of my cookies to take with you as long as you promise not to have any more until tomorrow." Maggie held up a warning finger before any of the girls could say anything. "And then only a few at a time." She looked from one girl to another. "Sandy, Christine, have we got a deal? We don't want you getting sick like Jennifer, now, do we?"

The girls solemnly shook their heads. "No," they both agreed.

Maggie saw the bemused look on Joe's face. Curious, she had to ask. "What?"

"You remembered their names." It was his job to remember people's names and he still managed to get them confused. Sandy and Christine looked so much alike, they were practically interchangeable to an outsider. Why would she remember who was who?

Maggie didn't understand why he would think that so unusual. "It's not as if you brought in the Mormon Tabernacle Choir with you. Just three little girls." Like flowers turning their faces toward the warm sun, the girls shifted their gaze toward Maggie, and she smiled at them. "My attention span can handle that."

"And a lot of other things as well, it seems." He didn't want to end it here. There was a host of questions he wanted to have answered. "Listen, we didn't exactly complete the interview—"

She was already walking him to the door. "Your editor told me that there was a deadline." That was one of the reasons she'd decided to agree to this. The deadline was soon. That meant there would be one interview and one interview only.

"There is. In a manner of speaking," he added vaguely.

As a fairly regular contributor of long standing, Joe was privy to the magazine's layout for next month. His mind was already juggling articles and working through negotiations. He could easily slip in another piece in place of the one on Maggie. He'd already done the legwork on it and all that was needed was a little polishing. Although the article was currently slotted for the following month, moving it up would leave him a window of time to work on this interview.

And he really wanted to work on this interview. In depth.

"But I think you'll agree that your interview was abruptly cut short and my piece still needs some fleshing out."

Something about the way he said that made her leery. "Isn't that where you come in? To flesh it out?"

He fervently wished the girls weren't here, hanging on every word, looking at Maggie as if she were the latest flavor of ice cream. Or chocolate chip cookie. "I need to know my subject a little better before I can do that. Could we continue this?—"

She shook her head, cutting him off. There were meetings to go to. She and Adam had one lined up with a new ad agency later this week. And there were the stock reports to review. "I'm sorry. My schedule's really full."

He was ready for her. "So my editor said. How about over dinner, then?"

She hadn't been prepared for that. "Dinner?"

"You know, the meal that comes before dessert?" He'd like that, he thought, having dinner with her. He'd like that a lot.

She looked at the girls. "Where? At Family Fun House?"

Joe shuddered at the name of the fast-food chain. It was where he went every time he took the girls out. An hour and a half of mediocre pizza, arcade games and ear-splitting noise.

"I was thinking of somewhere a little quieter. Like the Velvet Turtle on MacArthur," he suggested. Because she looked as if she would feel better as long as he kept it on a professional level, he handed her his business card. His home phone was on it. "Here's my card."

Christine looked up at him. "You gonna eat on a turtle, Uncle Joe?"

Joe's eyes skimmed over Maggie. He knew he wanted to see more of her, a lot more of her. The article was one reason, but it wasn't the only one. His interest had been aroused the moment he had looked at her. "If I have to."

Maggie closed her hand over the card he gave her. "I'll get back to you."

He smiled into her eyes just before he herded the girls out. "Please do."

His words hung in the air long after he'd left.

Chapter Three

Joe sighed and pushed himself away from his desk. The wheels of his chair snagged on the carpet, bringing him to an abrupt, jolting halt like a rider atop a stubborn horse that refused to go where he directed it. It was par for the course. The article wasn't going the way he wanted it to, either. Joe rose and shifted, realigning the wheels.

Sitting down again, he stared at the computer screen, frowning. Holes. There were large, gaping holes in this piece. He scrubbed a hand wearily over his face. Holes big enough to drive a moving van through and still have room for a circus truck to pass alongside it.

He reread the article he'd been working on since yesterday afternoon, scrolling down and hoping that it was actually better than he thought it was. It wasn't. If anything, it was worse.

He hated it. It read like an amateur piece found in some fawning, mindless magazine that wasn't worth the paper it was printed on. Certainly not the price of an issue. He wasn't looking to write an exposé, he just wanted to write a piece with substance. With teeth. A piece that you came away from knowing something. Not an article that read like lightweight fluff.

If he blew on it, it would probably float away.

Joe leaned back in his chair and rocked slowly, thinking. He needed more. A great deal more. He needed, he thought, what Maggie McGuire was hiding. Her past. Her childhood. Herself.

He flicked his thumb and forefinger at the white screen, discounting what was there. This was about as personal as a disposable plastic glove.

Sounds of infighting and squabbling vibrated into the open room. Joe groaned. He attempted to ignore it as he reached for the telephone. As of yet, there'd been no answers to the ad he had placed for a nanny. Not a single one. He wondered if nannies had suddenly fallen out of fashion or if he was just running a spate of bad luck. As soon as he had a chance, he was going to have to intensify his efforts to find one. He wasn't asking for much. Just someone with the patience of a saint and the endurance of General Schwarzkopf.

At the very least.

The commotion grew louder. He turned toward the doorway. "Girls, I'm working in here."

He'd only managed to tap out two numbers on the telephone keypad before Sandy, Christine and Jennifer came rushing into the room like the high tide, surrounding him on all three sides. For the rest of his life, he thought, they were going to outnumber him.

Joe sighed as Christine, always grasping for center stage, scrambled onto his knee as if he were a sofa, solely there for her use. He placed his arm around her before she had a chance to grab his shirt to steady herself on his lap.

"That wasn't an invitation to come in," he protested.

Christine looked at him innocently. "What's an in—an in—what you said?"

Sandy stood behind his chair, her mouth drawn in a customary somber line. She didn't laugh like the others, he thought. Two months and she still rarely smiled. She understood more than her sisters.

Her eyes held his now. "It means he doesn't want us."

The solemnity of the words jolted through him. "No," Joe corrected her quickly, firmly.

He placed his free hand on Sandy's shoulder, hoping that physical contact would somehow unlock the door and allow him to get through to her. Damn, but this was all so hard, so new to him. He kept tripping himself up when he least wanted to. His niece was hurting and he didn't know how to reach her.

"It doesn't mean I don't want you. I do want you, very much. Just not here in this room while I'm working." He searched her eyes to make certain that she understood the difference and was only half satisfied that she did. "It means I want you to be quiet." He looked around at all three faces. "Do you know what quiet is?"

Jennifer nodded just as she accidentally knocked down his crystal paperweight. It clattered against his metal wastebasket but miraculously didn't break. "No noise."

"Right. No noise." Shifting Christine onto the top of his desk, he leaned over to pick up the paperweight. He set it back on his desk, out of the reach of Jennifer and any further accidents. "Do you think you can make no noise for a while?"

Christine frowned and shook her head. She looked at her uncle as if he was babbling nonsense. "How can you make no noise? If you 'make it,' there has to be noise."

Joe laughed. He was going to be in big trouble once Christine began dating. "You I'm running for Congress."

He kissed her cheek and set Christine on the floor. He was aware of Sandy shifting farther back, making more room for her sister than the girl could possibly need.

Christine was still mulling over her uncle's words. She frowned, unable to come to a decision on her own. "Is that good?"

He liked the fact that they had such open, thirsty minds, but he wished they weren't so thirsty just now. He drew the telephone toward him again. "That depends on your point of view."

"View," Christine repeated as if she was literally digesting the word. It struck a chord. "Like what we did with that lady yesterday? Maggie," she added in case her uncle forgot.

"That was an interview." If he wasn't careful, he could lose an entire day like this. While he felt that it was ultimately good for the girls that they had moved in during the summer, giving them all time to adjust to the situation, he found himself really longing for fall and school. At least then he would have a chunk of the day to himself to get his work done.

"Look, girls, I really have to do some work here. I don't have time to play dictionary right now." They looked at him with wide, lustrous eyes full of questions. He cast around helplessly. "Isn't Big Bird on somewhere?" he asked Sandy. He had a cable television hookup with at least forty available channels. *One* of them had to be carrying a children's program.

Sandy didn't seem to hear the question. Her attention had been cornered by something else he had said. "When can we see her again?"

Her voice was so soft, Joe almost didn't hear her. He looked at Sandy, wondering what she was talking about. "Who?"

"That lady," Christine jumped in. "The one we saw yesterday. Maggie. The innerview."

"Interview." That was all Maggie McGuire would need, having them descend on her en masse again. "And we're not. At least—" he glanced at the screen and the article he was struggling with "—you're not."

As if they were somehow invisibly connected, all three small, round faces drooped simultaneously. She certainly must have made one hell of an impression on them, Joe decided. She'd made one on him, as well. A lady like that...

A lady like that was very good at being elusive and he needed more, he reminded himself. A writer was only as good as his next piece, which meant that so far, he wasn't very good.

"We'll talk about this later, okay?" He reached for the telephone.

Christine placed a hand over his, a little queen stopping a lowly subject. "But we're not on that, Uncle Joe. You can talk to us here, silly."

Joe remembered all the hard times he had inadvertently given his mother while he was growing up. It was too late to make amends. Mentally, he asked her forgiveness as he struggled for patience. He doubted that the girls understood that they were driving him crazy.

"I meant later. Right now, I have to talk to her. Maggie," he put in for their benefit. "Okay with you?"

Christine nodded. "Okay with me."

"Say hi!" Jennifer instructed eagerly. She grinned from ear to ear. "I like her."

Unable to help himself, he ruffled Jenny's hair. She curved into his hand like a small kitten responding to warmth. "I'll be sure to tell her that." He laughed. The cursor continued to blink demandingly on the screen, calling his attention back to it and his call. "Sandy, can you take the girls to the family room for me?"

The sweetness and light faded from Christine's face as storm clouds moved in. "She's not the boss of me." She jerked away when Sandy placed a hand on her shoulder.

By the time he did find a nanny for these girls, he was going to be worn-out and gray. "No, but I am and I'd like you to go to the family room for now. Turn something on. Watch TV."

Sandy nodded solemnly as she took Jenny's hand in hers. Not wanting to be outdone, or to appear as if she had capitulated, Christine flounced out before her sisters like a drum majorette leading a small parade.

Joe looked after them with no small measure of surprise. They were actually listening. In a way. A self-satisfied grin began to spread across his face as he settled back before the computer again.

"How about that?" he muttered in awe. "It worked. Maybe I can get the hang of this yet." The sound of small voices raised in a fresh argument floated back to him. He sighed. "And then again, maybe not."

He knew that he could rely on Christine to come running to him if any serious fighting broke out. A born informant, she enjoyed reporting on any of her sisters' wrongdoings. It was a perverse method, but at least it kept him on top of things. The girls were all basically good, just a little hyper. Or maybe, with the exception of Sandy, a lot.

Joe flipped through a sheaf of papers before finding the card he was looking for. Placing it on the desk in front of him, he tapped out the telephone number to Maggie's office.

It barely had time to ring once before Joe heard the receiver being lifted. "Ms. McGuire's office."

He pictured the dour-looking secretary. Frowning, he tried his best to sound gracious. "May I speak to her, please? This is Joe Sullivan." He heard the woman exhale loudly, as if taking the call had interrupted something of monumental importance. "It concerns our interview."

"Yes, I gathered that." She paused long enough for Joe to think that the connection had been lost. "I'm sorry, but Ms. McGuire is not in at the moment."

Her words were said entirely without emotion. He felt that he might as well be conversing with his computer. Joe wondered if the long pause was just for his benefit, or if she had checked with Maggie to see if the woman wanted to take the call.

Diplomatically, he forged on. "I see. And what moment will she be in?"

"It's difficult to say. Why don't I send along some more brochures for you to look at?"

He hadn't encountered resistance like this since his college days and the time that he had worked on a "tell all" magazine for the summer. The pieces hadn't been satisfying, but the experience had taught him to develop a tough hide. Maggie was stonewalling him. Her secretary had obviously been instructed to give him the runaround until he retreated.

It only served to reinforce his feelings that, despite her permission, Maggie McGuire didn't really want to be interviewed. That made him all the more interested in pursuing the interview.

Adrenaline began to pump as he smelled a story. "Sure, why not? Let me give you my address."

"I'll just direct it to your attention and forward it to the magazine," Ada countered.

She hung up before he had a chance to agree.

Joe let the receiver drop back into the cradle, far from satisfied, but far from stymied. The noise in the background had died down a little. He could hear a high-pitched, nasal voice counting to ten in a singsong cadence.

God bless public television, he thought as he tapped out the number to Magnificent Cookies' general switchboard. When the operator answered, Joe asked to speak to Ethan McGuire.

Every goal, he mused, had to have more than one road leading to it.

A sixties song floated through the receiver as he waited. Joe smiled. At least they agreed on music. He had no doubts that the selection was Maggie's. Though she had skillfully avoided answering any personal questions during the interview, he had come away with the impression that Maggie was involved in and aware of every single detail at the plant, right down to selecting the brand of paper towel used in the washrooms.

This time, he was put directly through to Ethan. "Hello, Mr. McGuire? This is Joe Sullivan. We met briefly yesterday. I was doing an interview with your sister—"

Ethan grinned, remembering. "The guy with the little blondes in tow."

"That's me." The last time that had been said of him, the reference had applied to blond models, not girls under four feet. How times had changed, he thought with an inward sigh.

Maggie had told Ethan that the interview had been concluded. If so, why was Sullivan calling him? "What can I do for you?"

"Well, I didn't have a chance to complete my interview yesterday. My niece—"

Ethan was ahead of him. "The littlest one threw up. Yes, I know. Maggie told me. I hope that isn't a reflection of what your niece thought of our product."

Joe wondered if everyone in Maggie's family finished sentences for the people they talked with. "I think it was more a case of her liking your product *too* much. But in any event, I'm trying to reach Ms. McGuire, and—"

"You can't." It wasn't a question.

Ethan knew that yesterday had been an aberration for his sister. When Sullivan had left and she had come to see him about the financial projections, she had looked immensely relieved, as if she had been through some sort of emotional ordeal.

He knew that was because of what she hadn't said rather than what she had. The whole thing mystified him. Ethan would have thought that Maggie would have been proud of the fact that she had managed to surmount her past and make something of herself. Of all of them, actually. There was no doubt that they were all where they were because of her efforts more than their own.

Instead, she was ashamed of it. She never said so in so many words, but she didn't have to. The fact that she didn't want to talk about their past, their roots, even with him, told Ethan that he was right.

"No, I can't. Your sister is quite a dynamic woman, and I'd like to do her justice in this article. In order to do that, I'm going to need more time with her. Her secretary tells me she's unavailable." Joe paused. The man could very well tell him to go to hell, but he didn't think he would. It was only a hunch, but his hunches were usually right. "Do you know where I can reach her?"

It was time, Ethan thought, that he took a little initiative himself. If the tables had been turned, he was certain that it would have been what Maggie would have done for him—whether or not he liked it. Maggie needed to divest herself of this cloak she had wrapped around their past. And Sullivan was the man to convince her to do it. It had been something Maggie had said that convinced him.

"She's at home today. Doing some work." He refrained from adding that Maggie was experimenting with a new mixture that she was hoping to put on the market in about a year. Maggie always tried things out first. "My sister does her best work at home, away from distractions."

That didn't surprise him. "I promise not to distract her for long. Is there a number where I can reach her?"

Ethan knew that he was going out on a limb and all but sawing it off behind himself, but there came a time when he had to use his own judgment instead of falling back on everything Maggie wanted. "Yes, let me give you her number."

It wasn't healthy for her to be as wrapped up in her work as she was, to the exclusion of everything else. She'd sacrificed her childhood for his benefit. His and Adam's and Richie's. He didn't want to see her lose the best years of her adult life sitting behind a desk and hovering over a stove, cut off from the mainstream of life. Cut off from the most im-

portant parts. It was time that his sister started living some
semblance of a normal life.

There was something about Joe Sullivan that Ethan found
likable and trustworthy. A man who brought his nieces
along on an interview because he had no place to leave them
couldn't be all bad.

Joe hadn't expected to get this lucky without really digging. "I'd appreciate that a great deal." He flipped over one
of the papers on his desk. As he reached for a pen, he heard
something crash in the family room. It didn't sound loud
enough to be the television set. Joe hoped that it wasn't
anything he had gotten attached to.

Ethan gave him Maggie's number. He sincerely hoped
that she would forgive him in time. This was for her own
good. He couldn't remember when Maggie had seen a man
socially, and while this one was only looking to complete an
interview, something told Ethan that there might be more at
play here, given a gentle nudge.

He could nudge with the best of them.

Joe felt a wide smile spread over his lips. "I'm in your
debt."

Ethan laughed. "I just might have to take you up on that
debt if Maggie goes after my scalp for giving this to you."

"I always protect my sources," Joe promised, amused.
He looked at the numbers he'd written down, making sure
he could read them later. His handwriting tended to be
barely legible when he wrote quickly. Joe darkened a seven
to distinguish it from the number one beside it. "Doesn't
like to talk about herself much, does she."

That was putting it mildly, Ethan thought. "I take it
that's a sign of your ability to understate."

"That's a sign of my pussyfooting around an issue until
I understand it better." Joe scribbled another note as it occurred to him. "Would you mind if I interview you about
her?"

Ethan wondered how Maggie would react to that. Maybe she wouldn't mind after she got rolling. And then again, maybe she would.

"Sure thing. Let me go over my schedule and I'll get back to you. One thing I can tell you now, she's a hell of a woman."

That wasn't just nepotism talking, Joe thought—he heard a great deal of affection in the man's voice. "That part I've already figured out for myself."

Five minutes later, after he had ascertained that nothing irreparable had been broken in the family room, Joe called the number Ethan had given him.

After four rings, he anticipated an answering machine switching on. None did. The telephone continued to ring. Maybe she didn't own an answering machine.

Because he had no other alternative, Joe held on for a little longer. Success, he always believed, came to those who had the patience to wait for it.

"Hello?"

Her voice was breathy, as if she had had to run to reach the telephone. It curled through his stomach like soft, wispy smoke.

Without realizing it, he leaned forward in his chair, his mind conjuring up an image of Maggie McGuire that matched her voice. It wasn't an image quite in keeping with the businesslike woman he'd met yesterday. He envisioned her with her hair flowing loosely around her shoulders. Bare shoulders, with moistened lips and—

Joe abruptly pulled himself up. He hadn't been out with a woman in more than two months, not since the girls had come to live with him. This had to be the equivalent of a diver getting the bends when he rose up too fast from the depths of the ocean.

"Hello, this is Joe Sullivan. I owe you dinner. And you owe me a few more words."

Maggie's hand tightened around the receiver. Behind her, in the kitchen, a fresh batch of cookies she'd been experimenting with were cooling on the rack, filling the air with a delicious aroma that would have set anyone's mouth watering. Maggie's mouth had gone dry. How had he gotten her number? "How about the word *no?*"

So much for rushing in and catching her off guard. "That wasn't the one I had in mind. As I said yesterday while making my ignoble retreat, I'd like to continue the interview."

She knew what he had said. And what she had said in response. But she'd had time to think about it. "I told you everything I intend to tell you, Mr. Sullivan."

The breathy woman was gone. The businesswoman had taken her place. Joe pushed on. "I know. Now I'd like to find out what you didn't intend to tell me."

She frowned as she turned around and crossed back to the stove. The telephone cord was twenty-five feet long and allowed her to move freely around her kitchen. "You're really making more out of it than there is."

"I'd like to be the judge of that. If you'd let me."

Pushy, but polite. It was a combination she would have admired if it weren't aimed in her direction. "I really don't—"

He'd gotten a little practice at this, listening to her and her brother. He jumped in before she could finish. "Do you have any plans for dinner tonight?"

Inherent honesty had Maggie answering before she thought better of it. "No, but—"

This was getting to be almost fun. "You do eat something other than cookies, don't you?" He leaned back in his chair and closed his eyes, summoning her image once more. "You couldn't have maintained a figure like that on fats and cholesterol."

Maggie smiled to herself. "You obviously didn't read the ingredients listed on the side of the box. My cookies are fat free, cholesterol free, low sodium and low in calories."

"A chocolate chip lover's dream come true." He recited the ad he'd seen in the Sunday supplement of the newspaper. "Yes, I know. I read the brochures you gave me. Several times. Still, off the record, you have to eat something more nutritious." Joe warmed to his subject. "I'd like to eat it with you. And talk a little."

Maggie eased the cookies from the baking tray with her spatula. Each one was a pale, perfect circle of flavor. She was going to have Adam round up a test group to try these out before she began congratulating herself, but something told her that she was going to successfully advance into the sugar cookie field very shortly. "Perfect."

That sounded much too easy. "What did you say?"

Maggie realized her mistake. "Oh, not you, I meant the cookies. I'm working on a new formula—"

"Yourself?"

Pride had her raising her chin, though there was no one to see it. "I take a very active part in everything that happens at the plant."

That much she had already told him. "Yes, I know. But about dinner—"

Maggie had no intentions of having dinner with him and "spilling" anything he might want spilled. "I really don't think—"

She was going to turn him down. He acted quickly. "Think of it as a favor to me."

Maggie set down the spatula, her attention sufficiently captured. "And why would I want to do you a favor?"

He was working without a net and he knew it. "Because you're fair."

He knew how to play this, she thought grudgingly. She switched off the oven. "And when did I say I was fair?"

"You didn't have to. You stopped to take care of a sick, frightened little girl you didn't even know. That told me more about you than anything you said. That's fair."

"That's instinct," she corrected him mechanically.

He had a feeling she was referring to more than just passing maternal instincts. He seized her comment, though he maintained a nonchalant tone. "Oh? How so?"

She threw him a crumb. "I raised my brothers."

Yesterday, she had mentioned that she helped raise her brothers. This put a slightly different light on it. Joe grinned. "See, you're getting more personal already. And it didn't hurt, did it?"

He made her laugh despite her feelings about what he was attempting to do. "I really didn't want to do this interview."

She didn't have to tell him that. He'd surmised as much. "I know."

"Was it that obvious?"

She was going to say yes, he could feel it. "I've had more personal answers from a swab of cotton."

The comparison was an honest one. At least he wasn't attempting to be obsequious. "And how often do you interview cotton?"

"Once was enough. You won't regret this. And who knows, I might be able to do you a favor sometime."

"Such as?"

"Give me time, I'll come up with something."

She had no doubts that Joe Sullivan could come up with a lot of things, not that she was going to give him the opportunity to try. She was too busy for anything he had in mind, including the interview. "I haven't said yes yet."

No, she hadn't. But she would. "Tell you what—I'll make you a deal you can't refuse. After I'm finished with the article, you can look it over before I turn it in. Anything you want to strike, consider it struck." He paused for a moment, waiting for her to say something. When she didn't, he added, "That includes me if you feel like it."

What would it hurt? She'd already held her own with him once. She could certainly do it again. And maybe, she admitted, she was just a little tired of eating alone. "You're very persuasive."

Bingo. He told himself not to feel too confident yet. She hadn't answered any of his questions. But that, too, would only be a matter of time. "Tell that to my nieces. I can't seem to persuade them to do anything."

She thought of the little girls she'd seen yesterday. Of the oldest and her sad eyes. Empathy whispered through Maggie. "They're still in shock."

He nodded. "Yeah, I know."

Well, she reasoned, he was obviously a decent man, and if she had final approval of the article, she really couldn't ask for anything more.

Except to be left alone.

"All right."

"Terrific." He felt positively buoyant. "Give me your address and I'll pick you up."

But Maggie had other ideas. "Tell you what—you give me yours and I'll meet you."

His laughter met her suggestion. "Not very trusting, are you."

No, she wasn't. But that was ingrained, thanks to her parents. "Cautious, Mr. Sullivan. The word is cautious."

Something else he was going to find out about, he thought, as he told Maggie his address.

Chapter Four

Maggie chastised herself as she drove down the long, winding street. What was she doing, agreeing to meet with Sullivan? There were important things that needed her attention.

But there were *always* things that needed her attention, Maggie mused, turning a corner. Still, what had possessed her to actually drive here from her home in Newport Beach and take Sullivan up on his invitation for dinner and inquisition was beyond her.

She slowed down in order to read the street sign. Deerfield. One more block.

Maybe she was doing it because she knew damn well that Sullivan wasn't about to give up until he had something. The look in Joe's eyes was familiar. She saw it in her own eyes whenever she looked in a mirror. It was the look of a person who wasn't about to give up going after something he wanted.

For some reason, Joe Sullivan wanted her. Or at least, a story about her. Maggie found Sullivan's street and guided her car down the long block.

She'd had Ada pick up a copy of *County Magazine* for her yesterday. Maggie had wanted to look through it and get a clearer idea of exactly what she was dealing with. The magazine was just what she had been led to believe it was: a middle-of-the-road journal, comfortably housed somewhere between the ones dissecting foreign policy and economics and the ones promising to cite ninety-seven different ways to bake a chicken.

Maggie smiled as she pulled up in Joe's driveway. She tended to lean toward the latter type of publication herself. Economics on a grand scale had a way of confusing her. She was only interested in the subject on a very personal level. It concerned her only as far as it affected the people she cared about and the people who worked for her at Magnificent Cookies.

Maggie pulled up the hand brake, then sat for a minute. Part of her wanted to leave now, before anyone knew she was here. She banked the impulse down, calling herself a coward.

Well, here went nothing.

She got out of her car and locked the door before slowly looking around. Sullivan lived in a modest one-story stucco-and-wood-trimmed house with neighbors on either side and a tall California pepper tree in the front. The ends of the branches were idly strumming along the tips of the grass on a lawn that was sorely in need of mowing, although small children weren't yet in danger of being lost in it.

Life, Maggie thought, looked as if it was getting away from Joe Sullivan. She could well sympathize with that. Only exercising the utmost control kept her on top of things.

It was the kind of house, she decided as she walked up the front path to the lightly stained wooden doors, that she might have pictured him living in if she had given it any thought.

What was still difficult for her to picture was the fact that Sullivan was caring for his nieces. He seemed like the type who might well have a female on each arm, but definitely the kind who were old enough to vote.

Maybe, she mused, sidestepping an overturned tricycle, that was what had prompted her to agree to a second interview. It wasn't that she believed he would relentlessly pursue her until he got the rest of his story. She was damn good at being unavailable, and what was he going to do? Swing into her house on a vine like Tarzan?

No, it was because he was faced with a situation that was so obviously not in his plans, the way she had been when her mother had died, when her father had abdicated his position as head of the house. It had stirred a feeling of empathy within Maggie.

It gave them something in common.

Maggie raised her hand, her finger poised over the doorbell. She never had a chance to make contact.

The door suddenly swung wide open. She had to shift her gaze down in order to see who had opened it for her.

Instead of Sullivan, Maggie found herself looking down at Christine.

Not standing on ceremony, Christine grabbed her visitor by the wrist and began to tug her into the living room. "We've been waiting for you."

"More like lying in wait," Maggie commented as she let herself be tugged.

Jennifer materialized out of nowhere, bouncing over to Maggie's other side. "We weren't lying down when we were waiting. We were standing up." She laughed at Maggie's words.

"My mistake." Maggie's mouth curved into a smile. Amused, she forgot to ask where Joe was. "It's an expression."

The living room lay directly before her. While not quite a mess, it wasn't that far from it. It was obvious that this was a place where children converged and played.

Jennifer tugged on Maggie's arm to get her attention. "What's a 'spression?"

"Expression," Christine corrected her, the way she'd heard her uncle do. "That's what's on your face, like the dumb one on yours."

She pointed an accusing finger at her sister's face, her own eyes slanting toward Maggie to see if the latter was being entertained by her cleverness. The mildly reproving look Maggie gave her answered Christine's question without words.

Maggie felt almost sorry for Joe. She placed a hand on Christine's shoulder and held her gaze.

"Christine, Jennifer's expression isn't dumb, it's just curious." Out of the corner of her eye, Maggie saw that the other little girl was now grinning from ear to ear, happy to be championed. "What would you do if Jennifer had said your expression was 'dumb'?"

That was easy enough to answer. Christine raised a very stubborn little chin. "I'd hit her."

Jennifer took a step back and Maggie knew that Christine's solution had probably been employed previously.

"Very honestly put." Maggie took a breath. This sort of behavior had to be nipped in the bud. That this was none of her concern vaguely filtered through her mind, but mediating this sort of a situation was as much a part of her as breathing. "So should Jennifer hit you?"

Indignation contorted the small face. "No, I'm bigger."

Now, there was reasoning for you. Maggie wondered how many nations subscribed to that theory. She ushered the girl over to the side and placed both hands on her shoulders. "Christine, my love, being bigger doesn't make you right. Neither does being nastier."

It didn't make any sense to Christine's young mind. Her mother had told her not to fight and Uncle Joe was always saying the same thing. But no one ever gave any reasons.

"Why not?"

Yup, definitely lawyer material, Maggie thought. "Because there's always someone bigger and nastier than you out there." She tried to keep a straight face. "You wouldn't want them ordering you around just because you were littler and sweeter, would you?"

Christine opened her mouth, but it was Jennifer who answered. "Christine is *never* sweet."

Christine swung around, wrenching out of Maggie's grasp. She looked as if she was ready to feed her fist to her sister. "I am so sweet!"

That was pushing it, Maggie thought, but the girl could be, given work. The main thing was that she had to stop being such a bully. Very gently, Maggie took hold of her again, bringing Christine's attention back to the heart of the discussion. "See, you don't like being thought of that way, do you?"

Christine let out a huge sigh and shook her head adamantly.

So far, so good. Maggie crossed her arms before her, resting her case. "So, how about trying to be nice to Jennifer?"

The connection remained unclear to Christine. "What for?"

Yes, Joe certainly did have his hands full. Maggie didn't envy him. This just reinforced her feelings about never getting caught up in this sort of way of life again. She'd had her fill of refereeing.

"For the sheer pleasure of it," Maggie coaxed. "She'll be nice back."

Christine still didn't see the real advantage in this kind of behavior. "She already is." Maggie looked at her expectantly. Christine stuck out her lower lip petulantly. "Oh, all right, I guess so."

Victory was victory, no matter how small or how it was arrived at. With a laugh, Maggie hugged Christine to her. Jennifer was quick to wiggle in under her arm as well, eager to snare a share of the hug.

A warm feeling filtered through Maggie. She absorbed it without consciously acknowledging it. "There, it's a start."

"I'm still nannyless. Any chance of you taking on the job?"

Maggie looked up sharply, releasing the two girls. Joe was leaning against the doorway leading out of the living room, observing her. He'd obviously been doing so for some time.

Embarrassed at being caught like this, she shook her head. A little of the poise Maggie had spent so much time cultivating returned. "Sorry, no way."

Joe entered the room. Sandy was behind him, shadowing his steps. Maggie wondered if the girl was doing it out of affection or need.

Or maybe it was just a way to protect herself and stay out of Christine's way.

Joe raised a brow as he crossed to her. Though she knew it was ridiculous, Maggie suddenly felt the room become a great deal smaller. "You say that with a lot of conviction."

Her smile was just the slightest bit mechanical. "I mean that with a lot of conviction." She glanced around at the girls and thought of the past. "I've served my time."

He nodded, remembering their conversation. She made it sound a little like a prison sentence. Was that how she felt? "With your brothers."

She inclined her head. She hadn't meant to mention that again. "With my brothers."

Any opening that he gave her, he was obviously going to have to push her through, he thought. For all her apparent friendliness, Maggie McGuire was the most closemouthed woman he'd ever encountered. He hadn't quite made up his mind if he considered that a positive attribute or not. He knew it was a definite detriment as far as his article went.

"Your parents worked?" He glanced toward the liquor cabinet and wondered if she would like a drink. Dinner was going to be unavoidably delayed, thanks to circumstances beyond his control.

There was a lot of that going on lately, he thought with a surge of helplessness he hated.

Maggie raised a brow, studying him. Sullivan was dressed very casually for a man she assumed was out to impress her. And there was a scent about him—not cologne, but something sweeter. Like some sort of cooking ingredient. Her curiosity was definitely aroused.

"You're not supposed to start asking questions until I've at least had a cocktail."

A drink it was. Joe opened the door to a small ebony liquor cabinet. His brother had brought the cabinet with him from Japan. Alec had given it to him as a gift last Christmas. Joe tried not to dwell on that. Coping was coming only in tiny increments, but life was to move on with.

He smiled as he looked at Maggie. "All right, what's your pleasure?"

The girls were clustered around her. Maggie had a premonition that they weren't about to leave any time soon. "Here?"

Joe nodded, one hand resting on the cabinet. "I'm afraid so."

Well, that explained the lack of the jacket and tie. "We're not going out to eat?" It didn't faze her. She felt more at ease here, surrounded by the girls, than she would at a restaurant.

Joe thought of the canceled dinner reservations. And the broken jar he'd just cleaned up from the kitchen floor. The jar that had contained everything that was needed for dinner. The same one that Jennifer had accidentally knocked off the counter five minutes ago.

"You know that line about the best-laid plans of mice and men?"

Maggie felt her lips curving in anticipation of his words. "Yes?"

He saw the amused sympathy in her eyes. "It applies doubly so to uncles."

Maggie read between the lines. It was certainly a good thing that he wasn't attempting to impress her. "No sitter."

"No sitter," he affirmed. "But not for lack of trying. So." He gestured toward the inside of the liquor cabinet. "What would you like to drink?"

Little girls or not, she wanted her wits about her. Sullivan was at his most charming when he seemed to be a hapless victim of circumstances, and she had a feeling that he knew it. "A little wine if you have any. Soda if you don't."

"Wine it is."

He reached into the cabinet as Jennifer piped up, "How about chocolate milk?"

That was even better, Maggie decided. She had a weakness for chocolate. "That's a great idea," she agreed, pleasing the little girl. Christine looked sulky because she hadn't suggested it first. Sandy, Maggie noted, said nothing. "I'd love some chocolate milk." She addressed her words to Sandy. "As a matter of fact, I love anything chocolate."

The thought of dipping himself in chocolate came flashing out of nowhere. Joe grinned widely as he poured a small glass of chocolate liqueur.

It was the kind of grin that put her on the alert. "What?"

This was neither the time nor the place to elaborate. Especially with his nieces around. Joe shook his head. "Private joke."

Maggie accepted the glass he handed her. "I respect that." She looked at him pointedly, raising the glass to her lips.

He watched her take a small sip and thought to himself that lips like hers were meant for finer things than merely talking or sipping liqueur. "And I should respect your privacy, right?"

Maggie raised her glass in a small toast. "You're very astute for a reporter."

He laughed, gleaning exactly what she thought of the press at large.

"I thought I was supposed to be, being a reporter. Which, by the way, I'm not." He thought of having a drink as well, then decided against it. He was making enough of a mess in the kitchen without anything fuzzing up his brain. "I'm a free-lance writer. There's a very large difference."

It was all one and the same to her. For the benefit of peace, she allowed him his differentiation. "I stand corrected."

"Would you like to sit corrected?" Joe gestured toward the large gray sofa. "Would you believe that only this morning, this was a castle where Princess Christine awaited rescue by her knight errant, otherwise known as Sandy?"

"Very easily." Maggie didn't blink an eye. "Gray is the right color for castles." Her answer instantly endeared her to the girls.

Maggie sat down, but when Joe tried to join her, he was unceremoniously elbowed out of the way by Jennifer and Christine. Like uneven bookends, they surrounded Maggie on two sides, sitting down beside her. Resigned, Joe sat down on the love seat. Sandy perched on one side of him.

There was a coffee table and three children between them, and yet, somehow it felt more intimate than she could have ever anticipated.

"I fully intend to respect your privacy, Maggie, but I do need to ask you for more than you've given me."

She raised her eyes to his as the liqueur wound through her stomach, moving slowly like a velvet stream. "All right."

He felt as if they weren't discussing the interview any longer. He realized at that moment that he wanted to get to know her better, not just for the sake of the article, but for his own sake, as well.

Except that he didn't have the luxury to explore that path right now. He had three small charges placed in his care and he owed them some sort of order and stability to make up for what they had gone through. This was definitely not the time to revert back to his carefree bachelor instincts.

He couldn't help wishing that Maggie McGuire had happened into his life at some different point in time.

Any other point in time.

Jennifer was rocking to and fro next to her, anxious to put her own two cents into the conversation. Maggie wondered if it was Sullivan's intention to conduct the rest of the interview here, over chocolate liqueur and fading gray castles.

"So we're not having dinner?" she guessed.

"Yes, we are," Christine told her. He was getting accustomed to the girls beating him to answers. "Uncle Joe is cooking."

Maggie looked at him dubiously. She could picture him in a kitchen even less than she could caring for three little girls. "You cook?"

He decided that she wasn't trying to be insulting, it just sounded that way. "I can turn on the oven. How hard can it be?"

She wondered if there was someone in his life who did the cooking for him, then told herself it was none of her business. "You're putting that in the present tense. Does that mean that you've never done it before?"

He lifted a shoulder vaguely. "I've warmed things up in the microwave."

And he was planning on making dinner? "That doesn't count."

"We have pizza a lot," Sandy confided loyally.

It was the first thing Maggie had heard the girl say since she'd arrived. She looked at Sandy, hoping to coax her out a little more. "And do you eat other take-out food a lot, too?"

The girl nodded her head.

Maggie turned toward Joe. "So what are we having tonight? Pizza?"

It was beginning to look that way. Most of what he had planned for dinner after a hurried trip to the grocery store with the girls was now residing on the bottom of his garbage pail. "Actually, I was making sweet and sour chicken."

"From a jar," Maggie guessed.

Again, he lifted his shoulders, hating the inept feeling he was experiencing. "Yes, until the jar had a sudden meeting with the floor."

She wondered if the girls had abruptly decided to play catch with it, but she didn't ask. The man was in need of rescuing, as, most likely, was her stomach if she let him continue with this charade. "If you let me rummage around your kitchen, I might be able to make the meal from scratch."

Joe's eyes narrowed. "You're kidding."

His reaction tickled her. She didn't know what came over her, but she winked at him. "Never about food."

God, but she had a sexy wink. "I always thought that when they said from scratch, it meant that you stood staring at the ingredients, scratching your head."

"You do if you never learned how to cook." Maggie rose. "So, take me to your kitchen."

The girls were more than happy to take her in hand and accommodate her. Maggie began to set her glass down, then thought better of it. The girls were far too inquisitive for her to chance leaving temptation in their path. She took the glass with her.

When she entered the kitchen, the first thing Maggie was aware of was that Sullivan obviously thought that every single pot had to be employed in order to be officially "cooking." The next thing she was aware of was the smell. Something was just about to burn.

"Smoke!" Jennifer cried, pointing.

"Steam," Maggie corrected her as she hurriedly crossed to the stove. She lifted the lid from the pot and a puff rose to meet her. It was the last of the water making a heated exit. Beneath the lid was a mass of rice, the grains glued tightly together like survivors clutching onto one another in a life raft.

She glanced at Joe suspiciously. "How much water did you put in?"

This was definitely not going well. "Enough, I thought."

"The rice obviously had a different opinion." Maggie lifted the pot from the burner and set it on the side of the stove. She turned the heat off and looked around. "Where's your apron?"

"Apron?" he repeated. Joe thought he was doing well just having pot holders.

Maggie shook her head. "Never mind. Where's the chicken?"

"I was just taking it out of the refrigerator." He opened the side-by-side appliance and took out a package of chicken cutlets.

At least they were defrosted. Maggie glanced at her watch. "Dinner was for seven, wasn't it?"

Christine spared him the embarrassment of a reply. "He got started late. We had to find Buffy."

Maggie nodded. "Of course you did." She looked at Sandy. "Buffy?"

"My cat," Jennifer proclaimed, wanting some attention. "She ran away."

Maggie glanced toward Joe and he nodded. He had spent the better part of two hours combing the neighborhood and knocking on people's door. Buffy was finally found curled up beneath his car in the garage, sound asleep. Reuniting a tearful Jennifer with her cat, Joe had hurried into the kitchen to begin preparations, only to have Jennifer climb up onto the counter and knock down the jar with the main ingredients.

The expression on Christine's face was smug and knowing. "That's 'cause you carry Buffy around all over the place and she doesn't like it."

Jennifer went toe to toe with her sister. "She does too."

Maggie moved between the two girls. "Why don't you let Buffy decide?" She looked from one girl to the other. "The next time she comes to you and nudges your arm, pick her up. If she doesn't do that, she's trying to tell you that she wants to be by herself. Cats are like that."

Sandy moved a little closer to Maggie, interested. "You have cats?"

As a child, Maggie had always wanted one. She would have loved any pet, but there was never any money to buy one. As she grew older, there had never been any time to devote to an animal.

"No, but I know some." Getting down to business, Maggie washed her hands and then began looking through Joe's cupboard. There had to be something she could do with that chicken.

"Really?" Christine's eyes grew large. "Do you talk to them?"

"Sometimes." Maggie frowned at the rice. There was no use in attempting to salvage it. It would only taste like burned rice. She glanced over her shoulder at Joe. "Never make the rice first."

He leaned a hip against the counter, content to watch as Maggie made herself at home and took over. "Why?"

"Because it'll be done faster than the chicken. You want it all prepared at the same time."

"I'd settle for it all being prepared in the same day." He gestured toward the counter and the banished pot of rice. "This is why I eat out a lot."

She took out the salt and the container of parmesan cheese. He probably used that on his pizza, she thought. Ingredients began lining the counter.

"Eating out a lot isn't healthy."

He handed her the skillet, wondering what she was going to make. "Maybe, but it's less irritating."

Maggie poured a little oil into the skillet. If he had an egg or some milk, they were in business.

He had both.

"Cooking doesn't have to be irritating. Or complicated."

The girls were arguing over who was going to help Maggie cook. Joe sighed as he looked in their direction. "Why not? Everything else is," he murmured.

Maggie took out a small bowl and poured the milk into it. "Got your hands full, don't you?"

"I'll say." The argument grew louder. "Girls, why don't you go to the family room and—"

Two out of three looked at him stubbornly. Only Sandy took a step out of the room.

"We don't want to watch telebision," Jennifer pouted. "We wanna stay here and watch you."

Maggie grinned. "I guess they know entertainment when they see it."

His eyes moved over her slowly. Yes, he thought, and so did he.

Chapter Five

To Joe's surprise, dinner was wonderful. Maggie had managed to create a meal out of things coexisting in his refrigerator that he would never have thought of mixing together. For once the girls had eaten without fussing over anything. The relatively tranquil atmosphere had allowed Joe to indulge in a second helping himself.

Maggie, he noticed, hardly ate at all. She seemed to derive pleasure out of watching the rest of them enjoy themselves. He wondered if this was how she approached life. Was she accustomed to remaining on the sidelines when it came to pleasure?

Joe placed his napkin on top of his empty plate. "You know, I really do feel guilty about this."

For little girls, they could certainly pack it away when they wanted to. It reminded Maggie of the way her brothers had always plowed through food, like a swarm of hungry red ants. In those days, it seemed as if there was never enough to eat.

Maggie stacked the empty vegetable bowl on top of the denuded chicken platter. "Then don't ask me any more questions."

He should have known she'd interpret his comment that way. He'd been too ambiguous. "No, I meant the dinner. I *have* to ask you questions." He moved his chair back, ready to take the plates to the kitchen where they would languish until he found the time to stack them in the dishwasher. Or until he ran out of dishes, whichever came first. "But I did invite you out for dinner and instead we wound up having it in, with you doing all the work."

"Not all." Maggie looked at the three girls sitting opposite her at the table. "I had help."

If they had beamed any harder, she would have had to put on her sunglasses.

That was another thing that had astonished Joe. Maggie had managed to get the girls coordinated to the point that not only weren't they a hindrance while she worked her subtle magic in his kitchen, but they were actually a help.

Granted, preparation had taken longer that way, but considering that the girls didn't argue nearly as much as they normally did, he thought of it as a more than adequate trade-off.

And the meal had been well worth waiting for.

Christine milked the moment. "Can we help you some more, Maggie?"

Maggie looked at the stack of dishes. The girls had to learn sometime, and she had the distinct feeling that no one had bothered to try to teach them before.

"That's just what I was thinking." Maggie looked from one eager face to the next. "Do you want to help me clear the table?"

Christine's face puckered up as she mulled the words over. "Clear it how? You mean pushing things off?"

Joe could readily visualize that happening. He'd had enough breakage for one day. He half rose in his seat, his hand over Maggie's. "You don't have to—"

There was something vaguely disquieting about his touch. Something she didn't have the time to explore. She waved his protest aside. Her eyes shifted to his nieces.

"No, I mean we're going to take the dishes off the table and carry them to the sink." Maggie rose, taking a dish in each hand. One apiece should do nicely for the girls now, she judged.

"I'm not primitive," Joe interjected. "We have a dishwasher."

She could remember dreaming about owning a dishwasher. It had been her most ardent wish each time she'd been elbow-deep in suds. Looking back now, Maggie realized that washing dishes by hand had had its moments. She and her brothers had spent a great deal of time talking around the sink.

Maggie shook her head, dismissing his implied suggestion. "Too impersonal."

She handed a plate to Christine and one to Jennifer. Sandy, following her lead, picked up her own. Maggie scooped up the two dishes she had stacked and, depositing her own plate and utensils on top, led the way into the kitchen.

"Some of the best memories I have," she related over her shoulder to Joe, "are of standing in the kitchen, washing dishes and drying them with my brothers. Gives you a chance to talk."

"Did you really dry a dish with your brother?" Jennifer looked up at her, obviously bewildered.

"Yes." Maggie placed her dishes in the sink, then took the ones the girls were holding.

Jennifer frowned. "Didn't it hurt him?"

Maggie bit her lower lip to keep from laughing. She was going to have to be careful how she constructed her sentences. Her mind tended to race ahead of her tongue, and while adults might be able to sort things out, children were very literal.

"No, I used a towel. I meant he was there to help me. They all were."

"How many brothers did you have?" Sandy asked her shyly.

Maggie made room for glasses, setting two aside on the counter. "Three."

"Like us." Jennifer grinned as she pointed to herself, then her sisters.

Maggie nodded. "Very much like you." She opened the cabinet beneath the sink and peered in. There was a prohibitive jumble of bottles and boxes under there. None of them looked particularly new. "Any dishwashing liquid?" She turned to look at Joe. "Or do you just let the cat lick them clean?"

The girls giggled, but Maggie hardly noticed. Joe was suddenly standing much too close to her as he crouched down and looked through the cabinet for the elusive bottle of detergent. His shoulder brushed against her leg, sending a jolt through Maggie that made her oblivious to everything else in the room.

She drew a small breath and prudently moved aside. Her leg continued to tingle. He looked up at her questioningly.

"Signal before you make a move next time," Maggie murmured.

Joe rose with a clear plastic bottle half filled with an off-yellow liquid that didn't look overly promising. "I'll do that." The words were innocuous. His smile wasn't. It held a promise.

He'd felt it, too, she thought. This was much more than she had initially bargained for when she had come here.

Maggie deliberately turned her back on him, stopped up the sink and began to fill it with water. Suds rose from the overly thick liquid she'd squeezed out.

Christine stood up on her toes, peering in at the bubbles that were multiplying. "We're really going to wash them?"

There was no missing the dismay in Christine's voice. "No, I'm going to wash them. You're going to dry them." She handed out kitchen towels to all three girls.

"And I get to observe?" Joe thought he knew her better than that already.

She lifted a brow in his direction. "You get the pots and pans."

Joe sighed dramatically for the girls' benefit, taking a seat at the kitchen table until his turn. "Knew there was a catch."

The kitchen sink was soon filled with soap bubbles and chatter. The girls seemed to be enjoying themselves even more than they did when they played video games. Then there was one endless squabble over the control pads. Right now, everything was going as smoothly as he could possibly hope for. The woman was a miracle worker.

He didn't even remember Julie, his sister-in-law, getting the girls to behave this well.

Maybe there was magic in those cookies of hers, the way the label claimed. There certainly was some sort of magic going on here.

The dishes took an inordinately long time to do, but finally, the last one was dried and put away. The last soap bubble had bitten the dust and dissolved by the time Joe placed one of the pots into the water.

"Can we go and watch telebision now?"

Jennifer was asking Maggie for permission instead of him. God, when the woman took over, she certainly left no question that she was in charge.

Maggie nodded. "You've earned it." She glanced at Joe for corroboration.

"No argument here." He looked down at the pot as it sank into the murky water. "Of course, you are deserting me in my time of need."

But the girls were already gone.

"Don't worry, I'm still here," Maggie assured him as she picked up a damp towel one of the girls had left behind.

"I'm counting on it." Cleaning was not his strong suit. Joe began to scrub the pot halfheartedly.

Maggie blew out a breath and elbowed him out of the way. "At this rate, you'll be here all night." She swiftly made short work of the dirty pot.

Feeling a lot like Tom Sawyer, Joe grinned as he picked up Maggie's towel. Maggie handed him the first dripping pot.

As he dried it, Joe studied her. "You know, this is a side of you that I didn't expect at all."

Curiosity rather than vanity prodded her. Maggie submerged the second pot. "Just what did you expect?"

He thought for a minute, remembering the short, crisp bio he'd read on her. "Oh, sort of a female Howard Hughes, both before and after." She looked at him, confused. "You know, high-powered, reclusive."

Reclusive? She was always in meetings, always on the grounds, talking to people, finding out firsthand how things were going. She had to be the least reclusive person on the face of the earth.

Maggie smiled as she looked at her hands, immersed in the water. "My nails aren't long enough."

He took the pot she handed him and wiped mechanically. "The rest of you doesn't look like old Howard, either."

Their eyes met for a moment, then Maggie looked away, reaching for the last pan on the counter. There was something very unsettling about the way he looked at her. "Thank you, I think."

The lady doesn't take personal compliments well, he observed. *Interesting.* "You're really something with the girls."

"The girls are really something," she countered with a smile.

Nothing but the sound of the television set was coming from the living room. They'd obviously been tired out. Another thing to bless her for. "No question about that."

Maggie glanced in Joe's direction and could almost see what he was thinking. "It just takes a little time, adjusting," she assured him. "It's never easy, raising children. And you never really stop worrying about them, even if they're not exactly your own."

He detected the slight wistful note in her voice. "Is that how it is with your brothers?"

There was something about being here tonight that was disarming. She usually wasn't this careless. "I was speaking figuratively."

"I wasn't." He laid the last pan aside and dropped the towel next to it. It slid, unnoticed, to the floor. "Tell me more about yourself, Maggie." He saw the same hesitation entering her eyes he had seen in her office. "Off the record."

She didn't like being explored like some foreign terrain. There'd been a time that she had been open, honest. And the people she had wanted as friends had ridiculed her. Ridiculed her parents, her clothes, her home. It had left an indelible mark on her and taught her, the hard way, to keep private things private.

Her eyes narrowed defensively. "Why?"

She looked as if she was ready for him to verbally attack, he thought. Why? "Because I'd like to know."

She shrugged a little too carelessly to satisfy him. "I told you everything of importance yesterday."

Then why did you come, Maggie? "No, you told me everything that could fit nicely into a thumbnail bio that could be found in *Who's Who*. You didn't tell me anything about Maggie the woman."

Maggie yanked out the rubber stopper from the sink. Water protested loudly as it gurgled down the drain. "Maggie the woman is a very private person."

Maggie the woman was a whiz with kids. Warm, friendly, as long as no one pointed it out. He took the stopper from her and set it aside. Joe placed his hands on her shoulders and gently turned her around to face him. "Why?"

With more dignity than Joe had ever witnessed, Maggie shrugged his hands off. "Because I just am. I led a very unsensational life before I began the company. No scandals, no lovers, no trading on the black market."

He knew she was being sarcastic, but she'd let something slip. "No lovers?"

Maggie frowned. That wasn't exactly the truth. "You were supposed to hone in on the other two."

He grinned easily, but he was unwilling to let the matter drop. "I'm an independent thinker. Like you." Because he suddenly had a need to touch her, he slid his hands along her bare arms and watched the pupils of her eyes grow large. "I zero in on what interests me."

Her expression hardened. "I thought you weren't writing for a tabloid."

This went beyond his assignment. "I'm not writing at all right now." He held up his hands to show the absence of a writing implement.

When he dropped them again, there was a hand on either side of her. And the sink was at her back. Maggie felt trapped.

There was something in her eyes he couldn't quite understand. Fear? Desire? He had no way to untangle it. "I know this is crazy, but I'm asking for myself."

Despite her wariness, her mouth curved. "Crazy?" she echoed. "That's not very flattering."

She'd misunderstood. "No, I mean it's crazy for me, because my life has never been as tangled up as it is right now." He combed his fingers through her hair, framing her face. "I don't have time to explore any new avenues suddenly opening up in front of me."

She should be pulling away. Why wasn't she pulling away? She didn't even know this man. "Nothing's opening up in front of you, Sullivan."

He would have been surprised if she hadn't protested. "Your opinion."

His words whispered along her lips just a moment before he lowered his mouth to hers.

The whisper became a shout, surrounding her like the din of a crowd in an uproar. Maggie completely lost all orientation.

This wasn't supposed to be happening.

The single thought telegraphed itself to her, echoing as if it were coming to her from a great distance, filtering through a tunnel. She was supposed to be getting back to the girls.

She was supposed to be in her kitchen, she insisted silently, experimenting with the new recipe, not in his, experimenting with fire.

That was what it felt like. Fire. Hot, crackling and overwhelming fire as his mouth slanted over hers. It felt as if she had fallen into one of her own ovens. Like the witch in Hansel and Gretel, Maggie was literally incinerating.

She couldn't break free. Worse, she didn't want to.

Her hands clutched at his forearms, gripping the hard muscles for balance, for support. For an anchor to reality.

It was curiosity with an overlay of strong physical attraction that had prompted him to kiss her. Desire had been a very remote third participant in the equation. Until it suddenly burst forward, taking over center stage.

Without conscious thought, only need, Joe deepened the kiss, not so much leading as being drawn in. Heat radiated from them both, seeking its mate. Joe molded his body to hers as he allowed himself to be abducted by the sensation that had risen so abruptly, swirling around them like a twister, taking them both out of Kansas and into Oz.

The thought that they were not alone, that he couldn't attempt to follow this to its natural conclusion, seared through his brain, pulling him back to Kansas. Back to his kitchen. And his life.

Joe moved away from Maggie, stepping back the way a person would from something he didn't quite understand and was just the slightest bit leery of. He wasn't aware that he had murmured the word, "Wow."

But she was.

She also slowly became aware of the fact that she was smiling. It was a reflexive action, brought on by something entirely beyond her own knowledge. Moistening her lips, Maggie ran a hand through her hair and prayed that she didn't look as shaken as she felt.

"If I could get that ingredient into my new cookie recipe, I'd say I had a winner on my hands." She hoped that sounded sufficiently flippant.

His hands had comfortably dropped to the swell of her hips. Something was definitely going on here, he thought. Something unexpected and compelling. Common sense would have him ignoring it, but he had never been one to pay too much heed to common sense. "We could work a little more on the formula."

Something akin to panic flared in her eyes before Maggie managed to harness it. "You have nieces in the other room."

When it was quiet like this, it usually meant that they had spent their enormous ration of energy and were settling down for the evening.

Joe lowered his head to kiss her again. "They don't fit into the formula."

Maggie moved her head to the side. "But they do. Very definitely."

As if to reinforce Maggie's point, Christine appeared in the entrance to the kitchen like a performer hitting her mark.

"Jennifer's falling asleep," she announced loudly. Her eyes moved back and forth from her uncle to Maggie like small blue tennis balls being lobbed over a net. She marched into the room, a miniature inquisitor. "Why are you holding her like that, Uncle Joe? Is Maggie going to fall down?"

Out of the mouths of babes, Maggie thought. Her knees did feel weak, not that she was about to admit that to anyone.

"Not at the moment," Joe answered. He released Maggie and dropped his hands to his sides.

Like a rabbit that suddenly had a steel trap open up around its leg, Maggie swiftly moved away from Joe, crossing to the sanctuary of the living room.

He didn't follow her. He needed a moment to himself, to assess what the hell had just happened.

The moment didn't help. He hadn't a clue. But he knew where to look for the answers.

When he entered the living room, Maggie was lifting a dozing Jennifer into her arms. Joe stepped around an up-ended car that belonged to one of Christine's fashion dolls. He reached for his niece. "Here, I'll take her."

Though this was something she had sworn to herself that she wanted no part of, she couldn't deny that holding a child in her arms felt very special.

"No, that's all right. She doesn't weigh much and she might wake up if I hand her over to you." Jennifer curled against Maggie, her breath warming Maggie's chest. "Where's her bedroom?"

"We all sleep together in one room. C'mon, I'll show you!" Christine volunteered eagerly.

Maggie laughed, following the little girl out. "I had no doubts."

Joe herded up the others, though there seemed to be little reason to. Neither girl looked as if she wanted to be drawn away from Maggie. He could identify with that.

"It's past all your bedtimes," he reminded the two girls as they walked into the room that had, until recently, been his den.

The room was crammed, with bunk beds lined up against one wall and a third bed catercornered beside it. A bureau and an overflowing toy box took up the rest of the space. As crowded as it was, the room was still larger than anything Maggie and her brothers had slept in when they were growing up.

Christine whirled around and hung on to her uncle's arm with both hands, trying to coax him into changing his mind. "Aw, Uncle Joe, can't we stay up a little longer? We don't want to go to bed like babies, do we?'' She looked toward Sandy for backup.

Sandy said nothing, but her expression was hopeful as she looked up at her uncle.

It was nine o'clock and Maggie had to be getting home. But she didn't want to leave Joe in the lurch. It wasn't her style. She laid Jennifer on her bed. ''You heard your uncle, girls. It's bedtime.''

Christine was silent for a moment, her eyes shrewd as she mulled over the situation. ''Okay, if you put us to bed.'' Her expression was almost coy. ''Will you?''

This was going a little too far. All Maggie wanted to do was to beat a hasty retreat home, especially after what had happened in the kitchen. She didn't want to hang around for something else to go wrong. She glanced at Joe's face. Really wrong.

It was time to go. ''I don't think—''

''Please,'' Sandy murmured behind her.

Maggie turned around to look at the girl. There was a mute entreaty in the girl's eyes. Maggie surrendered. ''All right.''

''And a story!'' Christine hurried to the toy box.

There were several piles of books scattered around its perimeter. Joe meant to build shelves for the girls when he found the time.

She was getting in deeper and deeper. Maggie began to think that she should have just turned around and gone home when Christine had answered the door. ''A story?''

''Yeah. A long one.'' Christine returned and presented Maggie with the biggest book she owned.

Maggie glanced down at it. The book looked to be the size of a large picture dictionary.

Maggie walked over to the pile and picked up another book. It was a book of fairy tales. Maggie made her a counter offer. ''A short one.''

Christine rocked back and forth on her toes. ''The whole book?''

Maggie glanced at Joe. He seemed to be enjoying this exchange. "She gets this from you, doesn't she."

He shrugged innocently, the corners of his eyes crinkling. "I haven't got the faintest idea what you mean."

Maggie held up her index finger. "One story," she told Christine firmly.

Christine looked as if she were about to be sent off to bed before supper without a crumb to eat. "Aw—"

This time, Maggie was not about to be roped in. She knew how this game went even without having played it out. "One story, after you brush your teeth and put on your pajamas." Christine opened her mouth to protest, but Maggie was faster. "Or I leave now. That's my final offer."

Christine knew when someone meant business. She darted to the drawer that Joe had cleared out as hers. "Where're my pj's?" She began rummaging through the drawer.

Sandy came up behind her. "Right here." She took the pajamas out and then picked out her own. Christine ran to the bathroom, claiming it first. Sandy sighed, turning toward the hall and the other bathroom.

"Jenny's are under her pillow." Sandy pointed to it for Maggie's benefit. "She likes to keep them there."

"Thank you," Maggie called after the girl.

Sandy left the room as Maggie lifted Jennifer's head and slowly pulled out the girl's nightgown. Laying it on the side, Maggie started to remove one of Jennifer's sneakers.

Joe joined her, taking off the other one. "You're pretty good at this," he commented softly.

She shrugged, peeling off Jennifer's socks. They felt damp and there was a dried smear of sweet and sour sauce on them. "Practice."

As Joe held Jennifer on the bed, Maggie took her dress off. "Your brothers again?"

She nodded. Working quickly, she slipped Jennifer's nightgown on.

Joe gently laid Jennifer down again, his eyes on Maggie. "I'd say that they had it pretty good, growing up with you."

There were times she doubted that her brothers thought that. Maggie tried to distance herself from the past as she folded the little girl's dress. "I had a lot to make up for."

Her reply raised more questions than it answered. "Why you?"

She shrugged, wishing the girls would return. "I was the oldest."

He wanted to understand. "Doesn't seem like much of a reason."

She sighed, remembering how many times she had ached for her brothers, ached for what they were deprived of. "It is if you care." She looked up at him sharply. "You're doing it again."

He set Jennifer's sneakers on the floor, dropping the socks next to them. "Doing what?"

Maggie picked up the socks and tied them together so they wouldn't be separated in the wash. It was an old habit. "Wheedling information out of me."

"I thought that I was making conversation."

She knew better and saw through his innocent pose. "You're a writer. You don't make conversation, you gather information."

When she tried to sidestep him, he placed his hands on her shoulders, holding her in place. "We all gather information, Maggie, about people who interest us. Or, in this case, fascinate us."

She looked over her shoulder at the little girl on the bed. "I'd say you had a lot on your plate already."

Why was she afraid to explore what was so obviously simmering between them? "I can always get a larger plate."

Maggie shook her head. "I'm afraid it would never be large enough."

Like the cavalry, Sandy and Christine returned, unwittingly coming to her rescue. Christine fairly bounced into the room. Only the telltale droop of her eyelids gave any indication that she might be ever so faintly tired. "We're ready!"

"Shh," Maggie chided, moving over toward them. "Jennifer's sleeping."

Jennifer's long lashes fluttered open. "No, I'm not."

Maggie laughed. "You little faker. You just didn't want to get undressed for bed, did you."

Jennifer gave her a sheepish smile. "I can't get the buttons right."

Maggie sat down beside Jennifer. The others clustered around her. "You only do that," she said, gathering Jennifer to her, "by practicing. Nobody ever gets things right the first time around."

Joe had his sincere doubts about that. He'd wager that Maggie got a great many things right the first time around. Just like the kiss they'd shared.

The one that was still inexplicably making his lips pulsate.

Chapter Six

Maggie slowly rose from the edge of Jennifer's bed, her eyes on the sleeping figure beneath the floral sheet.

Not a sound.

Carefully, she crossed to the bunk beds and looked at each occupant. Sandy and Christine were sleeping, as well. Maggie smiled to herself. Mission accomplished.

Setting the storybook down on top of the toy box, Maggie eased quietly out of the room and closed the door behind her. It had been years since she'd had to read anyone to sleep. Nostalgia nudged memories awake.

Almost like old times.

Maggie quickly shut the comfortable feeling out like a woman closing the blinds to block out the glaring sunlight. It seemed as if nostalgia was bent on tripping her up tonight. Every time she turned around, she was reminded of the past. She had no idea what had come over her.

Just what was she feeling nostalgic about? A time in her life when she had felt hopeless, trapped and alone despite her brothers? Or rather, *because* of her brothers? Because she was the only one who actually cared about them? They had been isolated, floating adrift. And she had been the bewildered captain whose responsibility it had been to somehow navigate them to a friendly port.

There were a million miles between then and now. A million hard-crossed miles. She wouldn't have returned to that period of her life for any amount of money and she knew it. If, once in a while, she missed the closeness that time necessitated, it passed.

Besides, she still had a long way to go before she could even consider becoming involved in anything remotely domestic again.

Maggie turned from the closed door and almost bumped into Joe. He was standing in the hall, obviously waiting for her to come out. He had two glasses of white wine in his hands. She wondered how long he'd been there.

She nodded at the glasses he was holding. "What's this?"

"Wine." Joe handed her a glass. He inclined his head toward the closed door. "Well, now that it's all quiet on the western front, I thought we might settle down for that interview." He threaded his arm around her shoulders and guided her toward the living room.

Maggie felt every nerve ending was at attention. Waiting. "With wine?"

He took a sip, watching her over the rim. "I wouldn't want your throat to get dry."

Maggie set the glass on the coffee table. "Small chance of that happening." She'd changed her mind. That little session in the kitchen had shown her that she was feeling much too vulnerable to do any more talking tonight.

He saw her looking around and guessed at the reason. She was looking for her purse. "You're reneging on your promise to do the interview, aren't you?"

She saw her purse peeking out from underneath the coffee table and stooped to pick it up. Rising, Maggie slipped the strap on her arm and then faced him.

"Not reneging," she corrected him. "We already had it, remember?"

If they had, he had slept through it. "When?"

He was crowding her again. Just by standing there, not even taking a step closer, he was somehow crowding her. She'd never known a man who could make air evaporate the way Joe seemed to be able to.

"During dinner."

He remembered every shred of the conversation they'd had over dinner. That had been far from an interview.

"Those were bits and pieces," he pointed out. "Mainly mine. You learned more about me than I did about you."

He had told her about his parents, now both gone, and the friendly rivalry that he and his brother had shared while growing up. He'd even told her about his work and been coaxed by Christine to show her the "shiny statue" he'd been awarded when one of his articles had been singled out as Most Insightful Magazine Interview of the Year. Joe had thought that talking about himself would put her more at ease and encourage her to exchange information in kind. It hadn't worked.

She smiled as she moved toward the front door. "That's how I do it."

He followed, mentally casting about for ways to make her remain a little longer. Her answer confused him. "You lost me."

He wanted to know about her. All right, she'd give him some more of her work ethic. "I learn all about the people I come in contact with. The people I work with. Getting personal helps them feel as if they're working for a friend. Most people try harder for friends."

He'd buy that, but her reasoning was flawed. "How can they feel as if they're getting personal if you won't tell them anything about yourself?"

Joe wouldn't understand. He'd told her about his family. He had had a mother who had opted to remain home to raise her sons and a father who had worked as a senior engineer in one company for twenty-six years, until he finally retired. Joe had no idea what it meant to come home from school and find your mother slumped over in a drunken stupor, her head pressed against a scarred kitchen table someone else had thrown out. Or to stay up late into the night, wondering when your father was coming home. *If* your father was coming home.

His parents had built up his self-esteem. Her parents had torn hers down. Maggie had given him as much of her background as she was going to give.

"I tell them enough." Her eyes warned him to retreat. "What I told you."

Seatmates on an airplane flight exchanged more intimate details than she had given him. There were huge gaps of her life that she had left out. What had inspired her? What had she been like in school?

"You should know better than to challenge a writer, Maggie." He set his glass down next to hers. "What's in your past that's such a big secret?"

A little of her smile faded. She raised her chin. The stance reminded him of Christine when she was being stubborn. "I'm not challenging you and it's not that big a deal. But it's *my* deal and I'd rather keep it that way." Maggie turned on her heel and crossed to the front door.

Joe followed her. "You don't have to leave, Maggie."

Wrong. "I'm afraid I do. I have an early morning tomorrow."

There was nothing to be gained by making her remain tonight. She wouldn't tell him anything. Her mind was made up. All he could do was try again tomorrow. Maybe she'd have time to think it over by then. "All right, how about dinner again?"

Maggie shook her head as she reached for the doorknob. "No."

Like the loud explosion of a firecracker, her flat refusal momentarily stunned him. Joe placed his hand over hers. He wasn't about to give up that easily. "Not that I don't think you're a fantastic cook. You are. But this time, I promise dinner will be in a real restaurant."

She shouldn't have come tonight in the first place. "Sorry, no."

In his own way, he was as tenacious as she was. "Lunch? I'll even make the sandwich."

She couldn't help laughing, but it didn't change anything. Maggie opened the door. "Tempting as that sounds, I'm afraid I'll have to decline."

Though she could always find ways to squeeze a few extra minutes into the day for something that needed doing, she knew that seeing Joe again just wouldn't be wise. She'd felt something when he'd kissed her earlier. Something she didn't want to feel again. Not because it wasn't wonderful, but because it was.

Maggie had her life all mapped out for the next few years. Nowhere on that map was there a detour that involved extensive socializing. Or extensive entanglements. And that was just what would wind up happening if she saw Joe Sullivan again. She'd be entangled. With him and his life. Look what had happened the two times she had been in his company. She'd cared for his sick niece, made dinner for him and read three little girls to sleep. That wasn't her. Not anymore. That wasn't part of the self-image she was trying to propagate.

Sullivan had a very persuasive manner and a very persuasive mouth. And she was not about to be seduced out of her senses and become involved with a man who had three children in his care. That was the kind of life she had left behind her. That was *not* the kind of life she wanted in front of her.

"There's no way I could change your mind?" he prodded, playing with the hoop at her ear.

Her mouth went dry. Maggie took a half step back, bumping into the doorjamb. She shook her head.

"This was the only free evening I had. Starting tomorrow, I'm teaching a six-week business course at the local college at night." She gained steam as she spoke. Initially, when she'd agreed to teach the course, she had had her doubts about taking on more work. Now she was glad of it. It gave her an excuse to turn him down. "Between that and my already tight schedule, I'm afraid that you are just going to have to make do with the details you already have."

Feeling in control again, she smiled and extended her hand to him. "It's been a very interesting evening, Mr. Sullivan."

He took her hand, enveloping it between his own. His eyes held hers. "It still doesn't have to end right now."

Maggie extricated her hand. She hated the feeling that she was fleeing, but it was very clearly there. "Oh, yes it does."

With that, she turned away and walked to her car, trying not to look as if she was hurrying.

Joe stood and watched Maggie disappear down the driveway. He sighed and shook his head as he closed the door. She was right. He could actually make do with what she'd given him. He was certainly skilled enough and creative enough to write an entertaining fifth installment using the sparse information she'd given him. There were ways of embellishing without resorting to fabrication.

The trouble was, he didn't want to write a piece like that. Not anymore. He wanted to forget about making this just the final installment in a well-received series. Instead, he was beginning to envision it as something more. A full article that could stand on its own, something that did more than just pay tribute and cite accomplishments. An article that told the public what made Maggie McGuire run.

He stared at the closed door, thinking of the woman who had all but flown out of his house.

What *did* make Maggie run? And why?

Joe spent most of the night thinking about the question he'd posed to himself. By morning he was no closer to an answer and no closer to how to make her talk to him, *really* talk to him.

After going through what had now become the morning routine with the girls, getting them dressed, fed and hopefully occupied, he faced his computer like a man who was drugged.

At least his brain felt that way.

He didn't need this.

He didn't need to go chasing after a woman who bulldozed her way through life, no matter how great her legs were. No matter how provocative her mouth had been beneath his.

Joe scrolled down the page, dissatisfaction nibbling at him. He'd been at this for half the morning and what he had down still didn't look good enough. Anyone could have gleaned as much from reading one of her brochures. It didn't begin to capture the essence of the person, both the driven business executive and the woman who had held his littlest niece in her arms while she gave an animated rendition of *Beauty and the Beast*.

No question about it, she was getting under his skin. That wasn't good.

Maggie had been right last night. He did have a full plate. An overflowing plate. He had three little girls to care for, provide for and raise. His brother and sister-in-law had left a sizable trust fund for the girls, but that didn't begin to cover their emotional needs. He certainly didn't want to get involved with someone now, especially someone who wasn't even receptive to the idea.

But if she wasn't receptive to the idea of becoming involved with him, why had she kissed him like that?

Damn, women should come with road maps and a book of instructions. Joe sighed and blew out a breath as he pushed himself away from his desk.

"Are you having trouble, Uncle Joe?"

Joe turned to see Sandy standing in the doorway. She looked hesitant about coming in, as if she was unsure whether or not she was welcome. A large stuffed rabbit, its body weakened from hours of hugging, was tucked under her arm.

He motioned his niece over to him. Joe had no doubts that Sandy was here seeking refuge from Christine's high-handed manner. "Yes."

A small smile spread over her lips as she crossed to him. Joe tucked one arm around her waist and drew her to him, settling her on his lap.

Sandy looked up at the computer and saw Maggie's name at the top of the screen. "Is this about Maggie?" She pointed to the article.

"Yes."

Sandy was silent for a moment, wondering if what she had to say would hurt her uncle's feelings. "Doesn't look like very much."

She was only looking at thirteen lines on the screen, but she'd inadvertently gotten to the heart of the problem, anyway. He nodded, looking at Sandy. "That's exactly what I was thinking."

Sandy knew her uncle had asked Maggie questions last night. Maybe he didn't ask her enough questions. "Are you going to invite her over again?"

A screen saver blanked out the monitor. Within moments, there were tiny tree frogs leaping over one another. Sandy stared at the screen, fascinated.

Joe curbed the urge to hit a key and banish the frogs. They were entertaining Sandy, and right now, they looked better than his article did. "I already did."

Sandy tore her eyes away from the frogs. "When is she coming?"

He made a note to himself on the pad he kept beside the computer. "She's not. She said she was too busy to come over."

"Oh." She paused for a moment, thinking. "Then why don't you go see her?" Sandy wiggled around on his lap to look at him. "You could wait until she was finished and talk to her then."

"No, I—" The protest died on his lips. He looked at Sandy and grinned. Some times it took a child to untangle things. "You know, you may have something there."

The smile that had been hovering on her lips bloomed. "Did I help?"

Joe kissed the top of her head. "Sandy, you always help." He scooted her off his lap and reached for the telephone. Sandy remained where she was, obviously torn between retreating and remaining. Joe saw her expression out of the corner of his eye. "Would you like to stay in here for a while and play?"

She nodded shyly.

Poor kid, Christine must have really given her a hard time today. Joe gestured widely around his cluttered bedroom. He had brought his desk in here when he had turned his den into a second bedroom for the girls. Between that, his bedroom furniture and the clothes that were strewn around—a showcase of his pitiful housekeeping abilities—there wasn't much room. She would have had a lot more space to play in either the family room or the living room.

Still, he knew that what she needed was to be away from the others. "Make yourself at home."

Sandy smiled and sank down on a pile of shirts he'd worn during the week that had yet to make it to the hamper. Within a few moments, she was talking in a hushed voice to the stuffed rabbit she'd brought with her, retreating happily into a make-believe world where there were no little sisters to make her feel inadequate.

Smiling to himself, Joe made the first of his telephone calls.

It had been one hell of a day. Joe mentally recapped it as he walked down the brightly lit second-floor corridor of the Humanities building at UCI. He scanned the numbers over the doorways.

With little effort, he'd managed to talk his editor into letting him expand the article on Maggie. That gave him more time and more of a reason to see her. It gave him the excuse he needed, not for her, but for himself. It assuaged that bit of his conscience that protested his even entertaining the idea of becoming involved with her at a time in his life when everything was unsettled.

Following his editor's stamp of approval, Joe had called Ethan and arranged for a telephone interview. Ethan had told him to call back in an hour. When he did, Ethan had been generous with his time. The information, though, was just as sparse as when Maggie had volunteered it. Joe had a feeling that Maggie might have cautioned him against saying too much.

What did come through was that, though she could be domineering at times—something Joe had more than suspected—Maggie was well-loved by everyone she came in contact with.

At the tail end of the interview, when Joe asked, Ethan had told him the name of the college where Maggie would be teaching that evening. Joe felt as if he'd struck pay dirt.

And then, to top it all off, an angel of mercy by the name of Mrs. Edna Phelps had turned up on his doorstep in answer to his ad for a nanny. She came with impeccable references that checked out and a grandmotherly manner that disarmed the girls.

She started tomorrow.

Tonight, she and the girls were getting acquainted, freeing Joe to pursue his skittish quarry. Luck was finally looking his way and smiling down on him, he thought, whistling.

Now, if it would only continue that way.

Joe walked to the far end of the hall. The door on his right was marked room 210. Number 214 was only two classrooms down. His fingers curved around the registration card he held in his hand. He had managed to get a late-admission slip for the adult education course Maggie was teaching.

He wondered how Maggie would feel about having an extra student in her class. If nothing else, observing her teach would give him further insight into the woman. And maybe he could finally get her to open up.

Joe stopped before 214. The door was closed. He opened it a crack. Maggie was standing in front of the room, writing something on the chalkboard. Joe opened the door and quietly slipped inside the room.

Maggie turned to greet the latecomer. The welcoming smile she wore froze and then melted, dripping away like an icicle in the spring sun.

Just what the hell did he think he was doing in here?

"I'm afraid you're in the wrong room." Her tone was frosty, accusing. A slight murmur went up in the room, but she ignored it.

Joe looked down at his registration card, then at her. He was the soul of cooperative innocence. His smile was almost beatific.

"No, room 214," he recited, reading his card. "New Business Opportunities for Women." He raised his eyes to hers. "This is the right place."

A wave of amused laughter met his assertion. Joe looked at the other people in the class for the first time and saw that, except for the picture of the president on the back wall, his was the only male face in the room.

Maggie raised a brow as she regarded him. "This is a class intended for women, Mr. Sullivan. Was there something that you failed to mention to me the last time we spoke?"

He waited for the laughter to die down. "No, but there was something that you didn't mention."

What? That she was entertaining notions of justifiable homicide? Maggie struggled to hold on to her temper. Instead, she maintained a calm facade. "What?"

"That you were prejudiced."

Maggie's eyes grew huge as she stared at him. "What?"

He spread his hands as if the issue was self-evident. "Well, you're ready to exclude me from the class because of my sex."

Maggie bit her lower lip and then pointed to an empty desk in the rear of the room. "Take a seat, Sullivan."

Joe inclined his head and made his way to the back. She had ceased to address him formally. Looked like things were heating up, he thought, pleased.

He nodded at the two women on either side of him as he took his seat. Settling in, he focused his attention on Maggie.

The look she gave him could have ignited the logs in three different fireplaces simultaneously. He didn't bother hiding his grin. If he aroused her anger, she might not be so tight-lipped around him. Angry people were less inclined to think their words through.

It didn't surprise Joe that Maggie gave a good lecture. Nothing, he was discovering, would really surprise him about Maggie McGuire as far as ability and determination went. Even without knowing her background, he could see the kind of woman she was. What he wanted to know was what sort of roots had prompted her to forge these paths for herself.

Was she taking after her father? Had he been someone who had encouraged his daughter to be all that she could be? Or had she done this to show him that women could succeed in the world just as well as a man? Had she had a strong female role model instead? Her mother? Her grandmother or a favorite aunt?

Or was she emulating Barbara Stanwyck from some old black-and-white movie she might have seen on television in the wee hours of the morning? These were the kinds of things he had to know.

She'd said that she had a lot to make up for with her brothers. Just what did that mean? Was she being philosophical? Or had there been something more to her comment?

Joe made a note to himself to talk to several people at the plant and get a few quotes to round out the article.

Shuffling noises brought his attention back to the classroom. Women were rising all around him, preparing to leave. Class was over.

Joe remained in his seat, waiting for the room to clear. It took a while. Everyone, it seemed, wanted a word with Maggie. Finally, the last woman walked out, leaving them alone.

The ease that Maggie had felt while she was teaching was instantly stripped away. She felt uncomfortable alone with Joe. Uncomfortable with herself, she realized. She began shoving her notes into her briefcase.

"You have enough time to talk to other people, I see. Why not me?"

"They're students," she pointed out. "And I allowed for that."

He nodded, accepting her reason. "Then you can talk to me."

Maggie glanced at the open door. "No, I—"

Joe held up the registration card. "Student, see?" He tucked the card back into the slim notebook he'd brought. "I'm one of those people you made an allowance for, remember?"

Maggie felt her anger flaring. "Why are you pursuing me like this?" She slammed the briefcase lid shut. "It won't be worth your while."

He snapped the locks for her, then smiled. "I'll be the judge of that. Besides, I find you very intriguing. You run a company, almost single-handedly according to your brother—"

She looked at him sharply. So that's what he was doing here. Ethan had told him where she was. "You talked to my brother?"

"Why?" He picked up her briefcase, intending to carry it for her to her car. "Is that forbidden?"

Maggie reclaimed it, annoyed that he was barging into her affairs this way. "No, you can talk to whomever you like.

He can talk to whomever he likes—" She was going to add, "—just not about me," but he didn't give her the chance.

"I'm sure the signers of the Constitution will be very happy you agree with their little notions about freedom of speech."

Maggie turned and, without another word, walked out. He hustled after her and caught up within a couple of strides.

"Funny thing, when I talked to Ethan, he left the same gaps that you did."

Maggie stopped and looked at him. "Gaps?"

It was time to stop playing this mental chess game. "Don't play innocent with me, Maggie." His voice echoed in the empty hall. "Unless you're all aliens from another planet, you didn't just 'happen' on the scene, full grown, five years ago."

"Ten," she corrected him. "It took ten years to get to this position."

"Ten," he repeated. "And since you're twenty-eight, that leaves eighteen years unaccounted for."

From the looks of it, they were the last two people in the building. It added to the nervousness forming in her stomach. Maggie began walking toward the stairwell. Joe remained at her side.

"I was born, I went to school, I grew up, I went to college. You already know which one. End of story."

He wasn't buying it. "If that was the end of the story, you would have said so to begin with."

Maggie opened the door and hurried down the stairs, the staccato beat of her heels on the metal stairs underlining her words. "I'm saying so now."

Encouraged by her temper, Joe pressed on. "Who were your parents?"

"They were two people who met and married." She reached the first floor and yanked the door open. She didn't bother holding it for him. "They're dead. Can we leave them be?"

That sounded as if she was covering for them, not herself. He grew more curious. "You're too young to be a product of the Rosenbergs." Joe beat her to the front door and turned around to block her exit. "What are you hiding?"

"I'm not hiding anything." She pushed past him and stepped out into the night air. It felt cool against her hot cheeks. She didn't stop to savor it. "It's just something I'd rather not remember."

Her car was parked a few feet away and she hurried toward it. For the time being, Joe let her go. He had enough material to use for tonight.

And there was always tomorrow.

Chapter Seven

Three weeks into teaching her course, Maggie began to feel that there were two things that she could definitely count on. Dusk would fall and Joe would turn up in her classroom.

Contrary to her hopes that he would abandon attempting to get that "extra something" for his article, Joe didn't miss a session. The class she gave was held every Tuesday and Thursday evening from six-thirty to nine. Sullivan was always the first to appear.

Though she had to admit that she looked forward to seeing him, Maggie was convinced that Joe was playing some sort of a mind game. He didn't hang around after class and ask her questions. Instead, other than nodding at her in passing, he didn't even stop to talk.

It was as if he had decided to wait her out.

He had a long wait ahead of him, she thought as she looked at him. Joe's head was bent and he was writing down something she had just said. If it was a matter of tenacity, she could hang on with the best of them.

After all, hadn't she done just that when everything looked bleak? When there had been no money for her to go to college and she had been faced with the very real task of finding a way to provide for her brothers, hadn't she managed to hang on? She'd found a way to make it all work. She had never let go of her dreams for them. Or for herself.

It had been far from easy. Maggie figured that she was approximately five years behind in her sleep, but that was something that she could always catch up on when things slowed down.

So far, that didn't look like anytime soon. Success had just as busy a schedule as poverty had. She was always hurrying on to the next project, always trying to get two things done while thinking of a third. Then she had done it to get a foothold; now she did it to maintain and nurture that foothold. And to make it grow.

True, she didn't stop to smell the roses, but there would always be more roses. There wouldn't always be more opportunities, not if she didn't make use of them when they occurred.

Which left her zero time for a personal life. That, too, would come later. Like the roses.

She glanced at her wristwatch and realized that she had gone over the class time by seven minutes. No one was rising. She supposed that it was a compliment on the fact that she had sufficiently captured their attention.

Either that, or they had all fallen asleep with their eyes open, she mused.

Maggie closed the folder that contained her notes. "That's it for tonight, class. I'll see you all next Tuesday."

As usual, several of the women came up to her with questions after class. Answering them, Maggie was very aware of Joe hanging back the way he had the first session. She felt herself tensing.

When the last woman had grasped her hand, telling her what an inspiration she was to them, Maggie barely murmured her thanks. Her eyes were on Joe.

As he approached, Maggie busied herself with gathering her things together. For once she wished that she weren't so organized and neat. There wasn't much for her hands to do.

He'd been hoping that she would come around, prompted by curiosity about his laid-back behavior, or perhaps even by a spark of desire. Neither had activated.

Something about the mountain crumbling at Muhammad's feet crossed his mind as he approached her. "I enjoyed your lecture."

"Thank you." She didn't look up.

He was going to have to go the whole nine yards. "Tuesday seems very far away, this being Thursday. Any chance of my seeing you Friday?"

He was asking her out. For the last three weeks, she had wondered why he hadn't said anything. Why he had given up his pursuit. It had frustrated her, making her feel deserted in an odd way. Now he was asking. It was like having the other shoe finally drop.

On her foot.

Maggie looked up as she snapped the locks on her briefcase shut. "No."

Obstinate as ever. "This isn't for the interview." He placed his hand over the briefcase. "This is for me, personally."

With a sharp snap of the wrist, she pulled the briefcase out from under his hand. Her smile was polite and distant. It would be a mistake to get involved. She knew that. So why was something wavering within her? "Even less of a chance, then."

He'd thought about her, fantasized about her and thrown all good sense to the winds. If she was going to turn him down, he needed to know her reasons. "Why?"

"I don't have the time."

The smile that rose to his lips, curving them sensuously, told Maggie that he felt he had caught her in a contradiction. "You just told the class to make time for the important things."

Maggie leaned back against the door and studied him, her expression incredulous. "Think a little highly of yourself, don't you?"

He shook his head. "I was thinking of that kiss we shared." As soon as he said it, he knew he'd struck a nerve. Good. "That felt pretty important to me." He cocked his head, his eyes holding hers. "Are you afraid of this, too?"

Her eyes narrowed, and she made him think of a warrior queen. A magnificent combination of sensuality, power and dignity.

"What 'too'?"

He shrugged innocently. "Well, you're afraid of the interview, afraid of letting anyone inside you. And now you're afraid of feeling like a woman." There was anger in her eyes. He fed the fire. "Your brothers say that you don't socialize."

So now he was trying different approaches to get his information? She had an uneasy feeling that Sullivan would somehow twist things around, making them even worse than they were. She didn't need adverse publicity. People who baked cookies came from pristine backgrounds, they didn't grow up in dysfunctional families.

"Leave my brothers out of this."

"They're big boys, Maggie. They can handle themselves. They don't need a muzzle to keep them from telling tales out of school. Truth is, they didn't tell me anything that I wanted to know, either." It was as if, by agreement, the past was a complete blank for all of them. His eyes swept over her, the slow, sensuous gaze lingering on her body, making her want to squirm. "What are you afraid they're going to tell me?"

"Nothing." She turned and walked out of the classroom. He was right beside her, the way she knew he'd be. So much for respites. "There's nothing to tell."

"That's what they said." His instincts told him otherwise. His instincts told him that her brothers weren't talking out of loyalty to Maggie, which ran incredibly high. If nothing else, the last couple of weeks' worth of interviews had shown him that everyone had a good word to say about Maggie. He must have spoken with fifty people, dealers and factory workers alike. There was genuine affection in their statements. And each came with some sort of personal recollection of her kindness. "My guess is that if you only had to get the votes from the people who worked for you, you'd be president of the country tomorrow."

She turned to look at him. "I don't want to be president. I just want to be left alone." Her voice echoed in the empty hallway. Turning, she continued walking down the corridor.

"Talk to me and you might get your wish." Although he doubted it. He'd thought about her too much in the last few weeks. She was too fascinating a woman to just walk away from after he finished working on his article.

She slanted a look toward him as she walked down the stairs. "You lulled me into a false sense of security, you know, not asking questions and biding your time. I really thought you were interested in what I had to say."

"I was. I am." He moved ahead of her to hold the passage door open. The first-floor corridor was deserted as well and only half the lights were on. He was glad she wasn't leaving alone. "I thought I'd see what there was to learn by watching you."

She didn't care what he learned. "And?"

"I learned a lot." He took her arm as they walked through the shadowy corridor. Maggie didn't want to like it as much as she did. "You're intelligent, savvy, and a hell of an attractive lady who should have a social life."

She turned toward him just as they walked out of the building. There were stars out tonight, and a bright, full moon. She wondered if he had ordered ahead for it. "And you're volunteering?"

The grin was slow as it moved over his lips, taking in every part of him. And drawing her in.

"Yes. Proximity has something to do with it, but I do seem to be the likely candidate."

Maggie looked at him as if he were giving himself too much credit. He used a different approach. One he knew was bound to get to her, even if she denied it. He was beginning to know her better than she wanted him to.

"The girls are asking for you." Which was true. If he hadn't had the article to concentrate on and had actually tried not to think about Maggie, his nieces would have kept her very much a part of his everyday life. "They want to know when you're coming back to read to them again."

She chose to ignore that. Maggie unlocked her car door. He'd parked, she noticed, almost next to her. "How are they?"

He smiled. They were finding a routine, he and the girls. It wasn't the most peaceful one, but with Mrs. Phelps's help, they were managing pretty well. "The same. Still fighting."

The word conjured up images. She thought of sad blue eyes. "And Sandy?"

He knew what she meant. "Still hanging back. I'm hoping that she'll come around eventually—if I can get Christine to stop picking on her long enough for Sandy to build up some self-esteem."

From what Maggie had observed of the girls, that would be no easy trick. She suddenly remembered the reason she had had dinner at his house instead of a restaurant. He'd shown up for every class. How had he managed?

"Who's with them now?" She shouldn't even be asking. The less she knew—about Sullivan, about his nieces—the better. If you knew, you became involved.

She didn't want to be involved.

"I have a new nanny for them." The relief he felt was evident in his eyes. "She's pretty good with them. Not like you, of course."

Maggie squelched the pleased feeling. "Flattery isn't going to get you anywhere." That's all it was, empty flattery. She opened her car door and tossed the briefcase in.

Joe placed his hand on the door, blocking her way. Watching her eyes, he ran the back of his hand along her cheek. God, but he wanted to touch her, to kiss her. To make love with her until one of them begged for mercy. "What *will* get me somewhere?"

She felt her eyes fluttering and she moved her head back. Or thought she did.

But when her eyes snapped opened once more, she hadn't moved an iota. "I wish you wouldn't do that."

Very slowly, he rubbed his thumb along the hollow of her cheek. "Why?"

Her breath was growing shallow. She liked this too much. "Because it bothers me."

It bothered him, too. A lot. He felt himself being aroused. "Good bother or bad bother?"

With effort, she took his wrist with both her hands and pushed him away. "Both."

They were on the cusp of something, something that he found himself wanting to explore. It seemed that the more she resisted, the more he was drawn to it. The excuse that he had the girls in his life now didn't seem to carry the weight it had earlier. If anything, it tipped the scale in her favor.

He smiled into her eyes as he cupped her face with his hands. "Then how do you feel about this?" He felt rather than saw the pulse in her throat throbbing just as he lowered his mouth to hers.

The very same explosion went off inside her, except that this time, it was that much louder, that much more mind melting.

Maggie was reeling from the first moment.

Whatever words she had used to keep him and herself at bay, to keep thoughts of him at bay, dissolved like a spider's web in a strong wind. She had no defenses against this feeling, no defenses against him, and it frightened her. Badly. She'd gotten where she had only through sheer control. The one time she'd let that control drop, she'd been hurt. Control over a situation, over herself, was everything.

And right now, she had nothing.

Nothing but this wondrous, pulsating feeling strumming magical fingers all through her, playing her as if she were the strings on a harp.

It had been three weeks since he'd kissed her. Three incredibly long weeks. Rather than fading with time, the memory of her mouth on his had intensified. It preyed on his mind, demanding to be satisfied, like a craving that wouldn't go away.

He'd thought himself almost possessed by the memory. The memory paled in comparison to the real thing. He felt his gut tightening as if a fist had been driven full force into it.

Damn, but he wanted her. Now.

He was shaky as he held her away from him, afraid of what he might be tempted to do. To push this to the point where neither one of them had a say in what was going to happen.

He knew very little about cooking, but he knew that if you raised the flame too high, too fast, you could burn the steak. It had to be cooked slowly, until it was ready to be savored.

Joe shook his head, his hands still on her arms. "You pack some wallop, McGuire." He waited a moment until he caught his breath. "There is most definitely something going on here worth looking into."

Maggie swallowed hard, wishing for a new moon instead of the steady stream of light that seemed to be flooding all around them. She wanted shadows to hide in. Gathering her scattered thoughts together, she shook her head.

"No mystery. Just hormones, plain and simple."

He was well acquainted with hormones. This was no knee-jerk hormonal reaction. There was a lot more going on, and he, for one, intended to discover what.

"They might be hormones, Maggie," he granted. "But there is nothing plain and simple about them." He didn't want her to leave. Yet they couldn't remain standing out here indefinitely, and she had already turned him down for tomorrow. He thought of the restaurants in the square across the street from the campus. "Are you up for a cup of coffee?"

She allowed herself a smile. "I'm not sure I'm up at all." Chagrined, Maggie glanced down. Her legs felt as if they were the consistency of gelatin at room temperature.

She was still standing. Standing pressed against Joe, with a whole squadron of pulses throbbing all through her.

He wanted her to himself a little longer. Anywhere. "There's a coffee shop just down the street. Metcalf's. They cater to kids pulling all-nighters. C'mon, one cup," he urged. "In a public place. What are you afraid of?"

Why did he continue to accuse her of being afraid? It rankled the self-image she had so painstakingly pieced together. "I'm not afraid. I just am not in the market for anything."

He placed his hand on her back as he ushered her into her car. "And I'm not selling anything."

"The hell you're not."

He only grinned in reply. "Just follow me. I'll lead you there."

"That's just what I'm afraid of," she murmured under her breath. She looked up sharply, but he didn't appear to have heard.

The coffee was excellent. And so was the company. In the dim atmosphere of Metcalf's, it was difficult to concentrate on anything other than the person sitting opposite you at the table.

Maggie spent an inordinate amount of time looking at her coffee.

"Can I ask just one question?" Even in this lighting, he saw the wary look entering her eyes. "I promise it's not about your parents."

That wasn't good enough. There were still places she didn't want him trespassing. "What?" She whispered the word guardedly.

He'd had time to observe her. She was beautiful, dynamic, and he could personally vouch that she was great with kids. It was only natural that her marital status raised questions.

He wanted to run his hand along hers, but refrained. Touching would only make him want to kiss her again. "Why isn't a woman like you married, or at the very least, spoken for?"

She hadn't heard that term for a long time. Maggie shrugged noncommittally. "I just haven't had the time. There's always so much to do."

He couldn't quite believe that she'd always walked alone. "There's never been anyone? No serious boyfriend, no relationship that fell by the wayside when you began your astronomically quick climb in the corporate world of chocolate chip cookies?"

Maggie avoided his eyes as she shrugged.

Her silence told him what he wanted to know. He'd suspected as much. Instantly, Joe felt the cold, sharp prick of jealousy. He hadn't the right, but he felt it, anyway.

"There was, wasn't there?" When she said nothing, he prodded. "When?"

She supposed that there was no harm in telling him this much. It didn't carry with it the taint of shame the way her childhood did. But when it was over, it had only reinforced it. "In college."

He leaned closer, effectively blocking out everyone else in the coffee shop. "What happened?"

Maggie tilted her empty cup and watched the remaining drop of thick liquid slowly coat the sides. "Nothing."

The hell it hadn't. "Did he break your heart, Maggie? Point him out and I'll shoot him for you."

His words were light, but the smile on his face was just a shade tight. There was a time, she thought, when she would have loved to have had a champion. Someone to do things for her, to make her feel safe and secure. But that was before she had done it for herself. Before she knew that she could only rely on herself. If you wanted a thing done...

She laughed. "No, he didn't break my heart. Bruised it a little, maybe." Looking back, she refused to attach that much importance to Jack. He'd done her a favor by showing her the error of her thinking. "I caught him with another woman. He told me he was going to be studying. He failed to explain that the lesson was in anatomy. Hers."

Joe nodded. "The classic story."

"Didn't feel very classic at the time." She set down her cup on the saucer. It was getting late.

He watched emotions play across her face and wondered if she was aware of them. Probably not. If she were, she would have found a way to seal them away. "So you swore off dating."

"Not really. I just didn't make the time for it." She didn't have the time to set herself up for more rejection. Her father and mother had set a precedent. And her experience with Jack had just cemented it.

Maggie frowned. Once again she'd told Sullivan more than she had intended. This was supposed to have been just a friendly little cup of coffee, not another stroll down memory lane.

Maybe that was why she was stonewalling him. She was afraid of getting hurt again. His smile was warm, sympathetic. "Don't you know that when you fall off a horse, you're supposed to get right back on again?"

Once had been enough for her. "I not only didn't get back on, the horse ran back to the stable, took a shower and died of old age. I don't intend to go 'riding' again for a long time."

"And that was the sum total of your dating life?"

"I already told you—" Maggie picked up her purse, but got no farther than that. His hand was on hers.

His mouth teased hers. "Maggie, for the good of humanity, as well as your own, I think I should ease you back into the process."

"*My* good," she echoed knowingly. "And your own?"

He placed a hand dramatically to his chest. "We martyrs never think of ourselves. It's against the rules."

She had to go before he made her want to stay. He was far too persuasive. Maggie began to rise. "I finished my coffee."

"I can get a refill." One hand on her wrist, he raised his other to signal for the waitress.

Maggie disengaged her hand from his. "Not tonight."

He leaned back. As far as he was concerned, he had already shown a great deal of patience and restraint. But he wasn't the only one concerned here. Obviously she needed more. "Then when?"

She didn't answer. Instead, she merely shook her head and began to leave.

He rose in his seat. "I'll call you," he promised, his voice following her out.

Maggie paused to look over her shoulder. "It isn't advisable."

With that, she left the coffee shop.

Joe signaled for the check. He smiled to himself as he looked after Maggie's departing figure. He was getting to her. It was slow going, but he was getting to her.

He was getting to her, she thought, half listening to the two children reading lines in her office. Damn, but he was getting to her.

Sullivan had no place in her thoughts, but here he was, sneaking in and throwing everything into a jumble, like a child standing up beneath a fully set dining room table, up-ending everything. She didn't have time to daydream about him. She had decisions to make, a commercial to okay.

Why was he doing this to her?

Maggie looked up and realized that Adam was speaking to her. From the sound of his tone, he was repeating himself.

"I'm sorry, what?"

Adam McGuire frowned. First his sister had taken complete control of the commercial away from him; now she seemed to be here in body only.

"I said, so, what do you think?" He nodded toward the two children. They had been listening to children read lines for the last two hours.

Maggie linked her arm through her brother's and turned him away from the people in the center of the conference room. "I think that I have never seen such a collection of artificial children in my life. Where did you get them?"

"The casting agent sent them over." His impatience was evident in his voice.

He was tired, she thought. Maybe he was carrying too much responsibility. She glanced again toward the children. The little girl's mother was fussing with her hair again. Maggie wondered if it was worse to have a mother who insisted on overseeing every tiny aspect of your life, or one who wasn't aware of any part of it.

The latter, a small voice whispered.

"They look as if they had all just been dropped from the latest sitcom." None of them had the sparkle, the personality, she was looking for.

Adam fervently wished that Maggie would go back to looking over Ethan's shoulder instead of his. "Some of them have an impressive list of credentials," he pointed out stubbornly.

That didn't impress her. She wanted naturals, not miniature adults who had to pretend to be children. "At six? I don't want a list of credentials, I want scraped knees. I want real kids."

Adam struggled to curb his temper. Ethan knew how to keep quiet when Maggie stuck her fingers into his pie. He wasn't as good as Ethan at shrugging it off. "Real kids aren't disciplined enough."

"No, but they can make the ordinary consumer believe…" She stopped and looked up at him. "What did you say?"

Adam blew out a breath. "When? I wasn't listening to me, either." Just as she clearly wasn't.

Why was he so annoyed? "I listen, Adam."

Adam shoved his hands into his pockets and turned to look out the window. There was nothing to see but parked cars. "Yeah, right."

He was chafing again. Lately, Adam had seemed unhappy, and she couldn't get to the heart of the reason. That bothered her. A great deal. Maggie always wanted to fix everything and make it right. There just never seemed to be enough bandages to go around.

But at the moment, they had an immediate, pressing problem to handle. Adam had signed up a film crew to begin work next Monday. "No, I meant, what did you say about discipline?"

"Real kids aren't disciplined enough," he repeated. Just what was she getting at?

Maggie grinned as she steepled her fingers together. "Perfect."

"I'd be happier about the compliment if I knew what you were talking about."

For a second she'd forgotten that he was even there. She looked at him as if he'd just roused her from a dream. "What? Oh. I have the perfect little girl for the commercial."

He looked down at the résumés he was holding and began to thumb through them. There hadn't been anyone who stood out as far as he was concerned. "Which one is she?"

Maggie shook her head as she glanced at the papers in his hand. "She's not here."

"Figures." They had seen several children yesterday afternoon. "You want a call back?"

Maggie was already out the door and on her way to her office. "No, I want a call first."

Adam followed. Though he was taller, he had to hustle just to keep up with her. "Maggie, talking to you is like trying to keep up with the Road Runner on megavitamins. What the hell are you talking about?"

Maggie sat down at her desk and drew the telephone to her. "Opportunity, I think." She had a gut feeling about this. Her gut feelings were hardly ever wrong.

Adam sighed and slumped down on the sofa. He was accustomed to sitting on the sidelines while Maggie did her thing. They all were. Someday, she was going to have enough confidence in them to let them do the work for her. At least some of it.

Until then, he was just going to have to be content to let Maggie be Maggie. It wasn't easy.

The telephone on the other end was ringing. Maggie braced herself for the sound of his voice.

"Sullivan."

She became all business, trying to bury the fact that even the sound of his voice stirred things within her. She was dealing with that. She could always deal with setbacks and obstacles. She just wasn't sure which category he fell into.

"How would you like to provide for Sandy's college fund?"

"Ever hear of the word hello?"

"Hello. So how would you like to provide for Sandy's college fund?"

"She's seven. I haven't really thought about it."

"Well, think about it." Maggie launched into her idea. "We're shooting a commercial next week and I need a little girl who's believable. I think using Sandy might be beneficial to her as well as to us." She was thinking of the girl's faded self-esteem. "Can you bring her over today?"

Here he'd been, knocking his head against the wall, and when he least expected it, luck threw him an ace. "I could."

She heard the contingency note in his voice. "But?"

"Let's make a deal first."

She sighed. Adam looked at her quizzically but she didn't stop to explain what was going on. "What do you want?"

"I think you know what I want."

Yes, she knew exactly what he wanted. Her privacy. "This is no time to haggle about the interview."

"On the contrary, this is the perfect time to haggle about the interview. I bring Sandy over, you pay her scale and I get my interview." He knew that something like this would make the girl feel better about herself. She was his first concern. But if it helped him out with a problem, so much the better. "Deal?"

"Bring her. We'll iron out the details."

"Deal?" he pressed.

Maggie gritted her teeth together. It wasn't as if she couldn't find someone else to play the part. But time was short and she knew Sandy was exactly what she was looking for. And she wanted to help the girl. Maggie sighed. "Deal."

Chapter Eight

"Don't look now, but they're back."

Ada made the announcement as if she were warning her about the return of a crew of aliens. Maggie didn't have to ask her who the "they" referred to. She knew.

Adam rose in anticipation of dismissal. He'd come in fifteen minutes ago in hopes of talking some sense into Maggie about the commercial. He'd had to wait his turn through a series of telephone calls. Maybe next time he'd take a number, he thought, the way they did at a bakery. It seemed rather appropriate.

Maggie put a hand out to stop him from leaving. "Wait. If this is who I think it is, I want you to meet her." Maggie was certain that once Adam met Sandy, he'd understand why she was so adamant. She nodded at Ada. "Send them in, please."

"Your funeral," Ada muttered, withdrawing.

Maybe, in a way, it was. But not the way Ada meant. Chaos she could take. Chaos she had learned to coexist with. This was something else. She was asking for trouble.

Common sense dictated that she work at pushing Joe Sullivan and his entourage out of her life, not find a way to reel them into it.

But there were times that instincts overruled common sense. Maggie thought this was one of those times. Sandy was better suited to the type of commercial she had envisioned than the mini-army of child actors and actresses she'd suffered through the last two days.

Adam nodded toward Ada's departing figure. "That didn't sound promising."

Maggie waved away Ada's comment. "Ada's just intimidated by anyone under five feet."

"That means you just barely made the cut." He grinned at her. Like his brothers, Adam was almost a foot taller than Maggie.

"Wise guy." She turned at the sound in the doorway. As soon as they entered, Maggie got the full inference behind Ada's tone. "They" were not two. "They" were four. Maggie had a definite feeling of déjà vu. Joe Sullivan came in herding three little girls before him. But this time, the look of wonder was absent from their faces. They just looked happy to see her.

It affected her more than she'd thought it would.

She had no idea that she'd missed them until she saw them again and felt the sudden wave of warmth flooding through her. It occurred simultaneously to her being engulfed by the girls.

Maggie raised her eyes to Joe, surprised. "You brought them all."

"I always said you were sharp." What adults couldn't accomplish, his nieces had, and with incredible ease. He had never felt outnumbered by women before. He certainly did now. "I had to. They're a set."

She was about to ask him what he was talking about when Christine, silent long enough, answered the question for her. The little girl made fists at her waist. "Why do you want to see just Sandy and not me?"

Maggie looked up at Joe and he merely spread his hands wide as he shrugged. When he had attempted to leave with only Sandy, the others had deserted Mrs. Phelps and the board game she was playing with them to demand to be taken along as well. Since Maggie hadn't specified *not* to bring the others along, he did.

"Not *us*," Jennifer corrected her sister stubbornly.

This one was not going to get lost in the shuffle, Maggie thought, looking at Jennifer. Sandy, however, was another story. She was already beginning to fade, like a shadow being engulfed by the long fingers of night.

Maggie allowed Christine to scramble onto her lap. She exchanged looks with Joe over the little girl's head and saw a small triumphant smile curving his mouth. He obviously thought she was feeling just as overwhelmed by them as he was. The man had a great deal to learn about coexisting with children.

"It's not that I don't want to see you," Maggie explained gently. Though her words were addressed to the other two, she was looking at Sandy. "It's just that I thought I could use Sandy in a commercial we're going to be making."

She looked toward Adam for confirmation. His expression remained blank. She thought he would have been convinced with just one look. Sandy had that innocent sweetness that they were looking for.

"A commercial?" Christine all but bounced out of her lap before resettling. Her attention was riveted to Maggie. "Like for toys?" Hope shimmered in every word.

"No, for my cookies."

"Me," Christine cried. "Use me."

Not to be outdone, Jennifer joined her voice to the plea. "No, use me."

Sandy said nothing, already taking for granted that her sisters would win the position away from her. Joe placed a protective arm around her and gave her a slight squeeze. He'd made a mistake bringing the others, but he hadn't wanted to get in the middle of playing favorites. It would have seemed that way to the others if he had refused to bring them along.

Maggie bit her lower lip, debating. Christine and Jennifer were both tugging on her, trying to persuade her to choose them. Not a single word came out of Sandy. Maggie reached out to the little girl. A hesitant smile rose to Sandy's lips as the girl linked her fingers with Maggie's.

"How about you, Sandy?" Maggie urged. "Nobody's asked you. Do you want to be in my commercial?"

"She doesn't have to be, we can," Christine insisted. A huff comprised equally of eagerness and impatience accompanied the words.

Maggie was kind, but firm. "I'm speaking to Sandy." Her eyes shifted back to the girl's face. "Do you, Sandy?"

Joe smiled to himself. There was a great deal about this high-powered business woman that he found attractive, and it went beyond the velvet texture of her mouth.

Sandy slowly nodded. Because Maggie seemed to be ignoring her sisters, so did she. "Yes."

That was all Maggie wanted to hear. "Adam? Do you have a copy of the script with you?"

This wasn't going to work, Adam thought. He saw the approaching fiasco in terms of dollars misspent. They were going to lose valuable studio time trying to coax a performance out of a girl who had to have each word almost physically pulled out of her mouth.

Adam handed the script to Maggie and bent over, whispering so that only she could hear him.

"Discipline, Maggie. Discipline." If she would only let him handle things the way he was supposed to, they could have avoided this disaster in the making.

Maggie refused to subscribe to Adam's negative attitude. "Enthusiasm, Adam. Enthusiasm," she pointed out. Being around the girls reminded her of years gone by, except that her brothers had been more like Christine and Jennifer. None of them had been withdrawn the way Sandy was. She had been the closest to that, inwardly. She had just never let anyone know. She never had the luxury of being able to hang back.

She thought of all she had managed to accomplish. Maybe not having the luxury to hang back had all been for the good. If she had hung back, none of this would've been possible. "You and the others had it, remember?"

He was far from convinced. Leaning over, Adam dug his knuckles into her desk. His voice was no longer a whisper. "We're talking about a commercial and a lot of money being spent."

She motioned him to the side. Flashing what could have been interpreted as an apologetic smile to Joe, she turned to Adam.

What had gotten into him? They never squabbled in front of people. If she had one firm rule, that was it. "Let me worry about that."

Adam sighed and shoved his hands into his pockets. For the most part, he was trying to curb the disappointment he felt. "You know, when you put me in charge of this project, Maggie, I had the feeling that you and I had different interpretations of what 'being in charge' meant."

What was he talking about? She placed a hand on his shoulder, stretching up a little to do so. Nostalgia bit into her. She could remember when he had to reach up to hold her hand. "It's a combined effort, Adam. Like everything else here."

"Combined," he echoed in muted disbelief. "Ten-ninety is not a combination, it's like the chocolate sprinkles on top of the ice cream cone."

She wished Adam hadn't picked his time so poorly. She didn't want Joe to think they were arguing. God knew what Joe would do with this scene when he wrote his article. She still couldn't shake the feeling that everything that transpired around him would find its way onto the written page. It wasn't helping her to relax.

"The sprinkles were always my favorite part," Maggie said easily. Before Adam could comment, she turned toward the girls again. She'd made her decision about the commercial. "So, you two want to be in this, too, do you?"

"Yes!" Christine and Jennifer shouted the word like two small stereo speakers.

It could be done.

Her eyes shifted to Joe. "Is it all right with you if we use them, as well?"

Him she asked, Adam thought. Why did a stranger she'd only known three weeks merit more consideration than her own brothers? Adam blew out a breath and decided that perhaps he was getting too edgy lately.

Joe was surprised that she had bothered to consult him. She was steamrolling over her own brothers. As it happened, if she could manage to use all three girls, that was fine with him. It meant one less bone of contention he'd have to referee.

"Hey, I'm only here for the ride. I'm still not certain just what is going on." He wasn't embarrassed to admit it.

Maggie ran her hand over Sandy's hair. "Adam, we haven't cast any of the other parts, have we?"

He had thought that they would pick the rest of the children they needed from the runners-up. He could see that, once again, he had thought wrong. "Except for the woman playing the teacher, no."

She knew that better than he did, he thought. As always, she was just thinking aloud when she brought him into things, using him as a sounding board. Usually that didn't bother him. But he'd just passed his twenty-fifth birthday and felt it was time he stopped being Maggie's shadow. He wanted to take on some responsibilities of his own.

Maggie nodded. "We're going to need two more consent forms for Joe to sign."

Joe exchanged looks with Adam. He saw the other's suppressed annoyance. It had to be hard, working with someone who attempted to do everything single-handedly.

It had to be worse when that someone was your own sister. Joe looked at Maggie. She was unaware of what she was doing, he realized. He knew her well enough now to know that she wouldn't have made her brother feel like an inadequate appendage on purpose.

There was no guarantee that if they became involved, she wouldn't do the same with him. What was he doing, getting mixed up with an emotional bulldozer?

"What am I signing?"

Her mind was racing ahead and she had to skid to a halt to focus on Joe's question. She would have thought the answer was self-evident. Maybe she was going too fast. "Permission to use the girls in the commercial."

Amid the squeals from the two youngest, he wanted to assure himself that he understood her intentions. "So you do want to use all three of them?"

"Yes." She placed an arm around Sandy. "Sandy still has the main speaking part, but there's space for a few extra children to be sitting around her in the classroom."

Christine stopped trying to wiggle in under Maggie's other arm. "We have to go to school?"

Maggie laughed at the horror on the girl's face. "Doesn't sound as appealing now, does it?" Christine shook her head. "It's just a pretend school. For the commercial."

"Oh." Christine stood digesting the information. "Okay." She said the word like a queen, giving permission to her subjects.

"Glad that meets with your approval," Maggie teased.

Adam gave a short laugh. "This one reminds me of you, Mag."

Adam's comparison surprised her. She could see by the expression on Sullivan's face that he agreed with her brother. Maggie opened her mouth to protest that there was a world of difference between her and an overly bossy six-year-old, then shut it again. She couldn't very well say that around Christine. But later, she and Adam were going to have a long talk. As for Joe Sullivan, she didn't care what he thought.

She slanted a glance toward him again, annoyed at the knowing look on his face. Business first, dressing downs later.

Maggie picked up the script from her desk, ushering Sandy over to the sofa. "Sandy, I'd like you to read a line for me."

"She doesn't read well," Christine interjected as she and Jennifer clustered around her again.

Nipping-in-the-bud time. Maggie looked down at the girl, her expression telling Christine that she meant business. "We'll practice."

Christine wasn't daunted. She tugged on Maggie's arm. "What about my line?"

"You don't have one." Her glance swept over both girls. "You just sit and look pretty." Maggie pointed toward the sofa.

Jennifer scrambled onto it, but Christine hung back. After a moment, she followed, although not too happily.

"I can do that."

Maggie smiled. "I had a feeling." She handed Sandy the script. "There isn't very much. Just the line marked in blue."

Sandy took the script in hand and looked down at the page. She took a deep breath. "Everything's better with a Mag—with a Mag—" Her cheeks began to turn red as she stumbled over the word.

"Magnificent," Maggie said gently. She squeezed her shoulder. "Yes, I know. It's a big word."

"That's like you," Christine pointed out, delighted that she had seen the similarity. She wanted Maggie to know how clever she was. "Maggie-nificent."

The word brought back memories for Adam. He was the one who had christened the cookies with that adjective when he was a little older than Christine. He'd meant it as the highest compliment for a sister who supplied all the love he'd known was missing. Maggie had provided love and cookies and he had felt secure.

"Actually," Adam began, drawing closer to the girls, "the cookie's named after Maggie. Magnificent was the closest word we could come up with."

His expression softened as he looked at his sister. She meant well, he told himself. It was just that at times it felt as if she meant too well. But then, if it hadn't been for her and her "conquer all" attitude, they would all have still been light years away from where they were now. Sometimes, when his impatience got the better of him, he forgot that.

Maggie smiled. The name had been Adam's idea. She had been against it initially, but he and Ethan had persuaded her. Richie thought it was a great joke, but then, to Richie, everything was laced with humor. She'd seen to that. She'd striven more than half her life to make sure that they weren't touched by insecurities, the way she had been.

"Never mind how the cookie got its name." She gave Sandy a hug. "Okay, can we try it again?"

Sandy nodded. She held the script firmly in both hands, as if she was afraid it would fly away from her if she released it. Taking another deep breath, she repeated the line with feeling.

"Everything's better with a Magnificent—" she looked up at Maggie, proud of herself for getting it right "—chocolate Chip Cookie inside." Her eyes were hopeful, hungry for approval as she looked up again.

Maggie felt pride weaving through her with bold stitches. "You're a natural, honey."

Sandy looked undecided whether or not that was good. "A natural what?"

"She means you have natural talent," Joe explained. He was surprised that she didn't read the words haltingly. Maybe Maggie was on to something here.

"Exactly." Maggie looked over her shoulder at Adam, waiting for his input.

He had no trouble admitting he was wrong, especially when it seemed to make everyone so happy. "Okay, you were right. She sounds better cold than most of the other little thespians we had trooping through."

"What are *those?*" Jennifer shivered, envisioning some sort of monsters.

"Actors, Jenny, would-be actors," Maggie explained before Joe had a chance to answer his niece. She turned toward him. "All we need is your approval via your signature on the consent forms and we're in business." Joe could see that the girls thought his agreement was a foregone conclusion. He grinned, holding out for just a second.

"I have a feeling, Maggie McGuire, that you don't need anyone's approval to be in business." If there had been any lingering doubts, Adam's laugh dispelled them. Maggie looked at Joe pointedly and he held his hands up in surrender. "Where are the papers? I'll sign."

Christine made one last pitch. "Are you sure we don't get to talk?"

Maggie pretended to look over the pages in the script. "I'm afraid not."

"Then I'll really sign." Joe laughed as he ruffled Christine's hair.

She tossed her head indignantly and smoothed down her hair. "Uncle Joe!"

Sandy beamed. Joe looked at Maggie. "I appreciate this."

His words warmed her, like a burst of warm air after a long walk on a wintry night. She shook it off.

"I wasn't doing it for you," she pointed out firmly as Adam left to get the consent forms.

"I still appreciate this."

She merely nodded and turned her attention to the girls, refusing to acknowledge the strange knot in her stomach.

With the principal participants of the commercial signed, there was nothing to impede the filming. Studio space, thanks to a few phone calls, was on standby. Shooting began early in the morning.

Maggie postponed a scheduled meeting so she could be on the set to smooth over any problems that might arise with the girls. Adam had expected nothing less, though he had hoped for a free hand.

The commercial, as she had envisioned it, was a simple scene within a classroom. Outside, there was a steady stream of rain, inside, the steady drone of a teacher's voice. The camera shifted to several children before it finally closed in on Sandy.

The little girl slowly burrowed her hand into her backpack and pulled out a bright red sack with the words Magnificent Chocolate Chip Cookies emblazoned on it in pristine white. She took one out and bit into it.

Instantly, the classroom disappeared and she was on a playground, surrounded with laughing children. Sunshine poured over the scene. Sandy delivered her line.

After some rehearsal and twenty-three takes, the scene was completed.

"I never knew commercials took so long to film," Joe commented. "Hey, you're as tense as an ironing board."

"It might have something to do with the fact that you've got your arm where you shouldn't," Maggie countered.

"Flattering as that is, I don't think so." He glanced toward his niece. "That's vicarious tension. You're worried about Sandy."

"Maybe I see myself in her." She bit her lip, realizing that she'd slipped. "Watch the commercial."

After twenty-three takes, he knew it by heart. "I don't have to. If I shut my eyes, I see it all over and over again." He looked down at her. "I'd rather look at you and imprint that on my brain cells."

Maggie shrugged him off and moved away. A deep, sensuous laugh followed her.

When the director announced, "Cut and print," there was an appreciative, relieved round of applause.

Sandy looked bewildered at first, and then smiled shyly.

Maggie was the first to reach her. She hugged the little girl. Christine, enthused, announced, "Group hug!"

In the blink of an eye, Maggie found herself in the center of a crowd scene. There were three sets of small arms hugging her. But what she was keenly aware of was the one set of large, muscular ones.

Trying vainly not to react to him, Maggie looked at Joe questioningly.

"She said group hug," he answered innocently. He looked down at Sandy. It was the happiest, he thought, that he had seen his oldest niece in a long time.

It was safer, Maggie decided, looking at Sandy. "You were wonderful."

Adam laid a hand on his sister's shoulder. The girls broke ranks around her. "When you're right, you're right."

Maggie almost said, "I usually am," but refrained. The comparison he'd made between her and Christine still lingered in her mind. Maybe she *had* gotten too domineering. She always wanted the best for them, for everyone. She was aware that at times it made her usurp everyone's rights in a situation.

Her smile was genuine and grateful. "Thanks."

Christine marched back onto the set, taking the seat Sandy had vacated. "Now it's my turn. Action, camera!" She looked around expectantly. No one moved.

Maggie crossed to her and took Christine firmly by the hand. "I'm afraid that it isn't your turn."

Christine's lower lip protruded. "We can't trade places?"

"No, Sandy had the starring role. And she was very good at it. You were good in your parts, too." Jennifer seemed to accept the praise, but Christine was still unconvinced. Maggie cupped the girl's chin in her hand. "The commercial wouldn't have been any good without you. You played a very important part."

"But we just sat." She looked up at her uncle for support.

"It's Maggie's show, Christine. You can't tell everyone what to do," Joe pointed out.

It wasn't what Christine wanted to hear.

Maggie placed her hands on the slumped shoulders and turned the girl toward her. "You made the people watching believe it was a classroom, and then a playground. Without you, it wouldn't have been believable." She dropped her hands from Christine's shoulders. "And Sandy said the lines that will sell more cookies for us." She didn't want to promote a schism between the girls. She just wanted to bolster Sandy's self-confidence. "You'll understand what I'm saying a lot better if you see it."

Looking around, she saw Adam talking to the director. "George, is there any chance we can see the commercial now?"

The director spread his hands in a shrug. "Only the roughest cut."

"Fine. That's all we need. We're not fussy," Maggie assured him.

Like hell she wasn't. Joe could see the same thought running across Adam's mind.

"Now *there,*" Joe said, placing a hand on her shoulder, "is what we call a contradiction."

Maggie looked genuinely surprised at the assessment. She didn't think of herself as fussy. Fussy people were difficult to live with. She just wanted the best for everyone.

"Me? Fussy?"

Joe nodded. His hand remained where it was. "About every detail in your life."

So, he thought he had her number, did he? "Got that from watching me in class, did you?"

"Got that from watching you, period." He dropped his hand to his side as she moved to accept the videotape from the cameraman. He knew that she would conveniently forget about the interview if given half a chance. "By the way, after we watch the rushes—"

She knew what was coming. Because of all the excitement, she'd hoped for at least a postponement. Apparently not. "Yes?"

"You have to pay the piper."

She blew out a breath. "More like giving the devil his due."

Her disgruntled comment had no effect on him. "Whatever metaphor pleases you, as long as you answer my questions."

A fragment of a memory nudged its way forward. "I thought you had to get the article out in a hurry."

He nodded. "I did—"

Maggie frowned. "Three weeks doesn't seem like much of a hurry."

He'd neglected to tell her, knowing that she would balk at it. "That was before I talked my editor into making you a feature story for the next issue."

Oh, damn, this was even worse than she thought. She should have never made this bargain with him. "Why do I suddenly feel like Faust at the stroke of midnight?"

"I haven't the faintest idea." Despite the fact that they were on a sound stage with a fair amount of people around them, he made her feel as if they were completely alone when he took her hand into his. His manner was warm, coaxing. "Maggie, I'm on your side."

She broke contact; it didn't help. She still felt his hand on hers. "I doubt it. My side doesn't want an interview of any sort. My side just wants a little good publicity to help me push a few more boxes of cookies."

Joe had done his research. He'd seen the last quarters' sales figures. And that was before her chocolate chip bouquets had gone on the market, cookies arranged like long-stemmed roses and sold as gift items in select department stores. He'd heard that they were doing phenomenally well.

Joe laughed. "Now, there is a *real* understatement."

Maggic ignored him as she motioned the girls to follow her to a screening room. "Let's watch what real teamwork can do, girls."

"Maybe you can take notes," Adam whispered.

When she looked up, her brother was smiling. But she knew that he was serious.

Chapter Nine

Christine rushed ahead of the others to the first row of the small screening room. She looked around in awe.

"This is just like when we go to the movies." To reinforce her observation, Christine expectantly pushed one of the seats down. It snapped back into place. Jennifer giggled. Provided with an audience, Christine pushed the seat down and released it again.

With a suppressed sigh, Joe caught Christine's hand before she could attempt a third try. "It's called a screening room. This is where we're going to watch the commercial you just did. Provided you don't break any of the seats."

Christine appeared sufficiently chastised, at least for the moment.

"Can we have popcorn?" Jennifer asked.

"We're not going to be here that long." Maggie thought that explanation was easier than going into *why* there was no popcorn.

Maggie led the way into an aisle, her hand firmly wrapped around Sandy's. Joe followed with the other girls. Adam remained with the projectionist.

Joe couldn't help thinking how much this resembled a family outing. He wondered what Maggie would say if he pointed that out to her.

Or if he told her how much she seemed to fit into the structure of his newly formed family. How much he wanted her to fit in.

"I can eat fast," Jennifer persisted. Movie theaters of any size meant popcorn to Jennifer.

Maggie thought of their first meeting. "Yes, I know. And I know what happens when you do." She looked down the row to make sure that everyone was seated. A moment later, the room darkened.

Jennifer started to say something again, but Maggie cut her off. "Shh. Watch. This is what I mean by teamwork."

The girls watched as the sixty-second commercial breezed by. Exclamations of wonder and glee at seeing themselves enlarged to such gigantic proportions accompanied the showing.

The lights went up. Maggie sat forward as she turned to look at the others. "Well?"

"I really *am* a big girl," Jennifer cried, pleased.

Christine wiggled in her seat, giving the impression of a lid about to be propelled off a boiling pot. "Can we see it again?"

Sandy remained pensively quiet, digesting what she had just watched. Maybe she needed to watch herself again, Maggie thought.

She nodded. "Once more." She turned around in her seat, looking toward the rear of the small room. "They want to see it again."

Adam signaled the projectionist in the glass booth to rewind. Moments later, the room was dark again, except for the larger-than-life images on the screen.

In another minute, the commercial faded into a series of numbers. "We'd better leave," Maggie urged. "There's still a lot of editing work to be done with the commercial before it can air."

As soon as they filed out of the row, Christine turned to look at Maggie. "Are all those dots and arrows going to be in it, too?" She didn't think they were very pretty.

"No, that goes out with the editing. That's part of the work they still have to do." Maggie paused before the door, wanting to hear the girls' reactions. "So, do you see what I mean about teamwork?"

"I *was* good, wasn't I?" Christine preened like a prima donna in the making.

The lesson seemed to have fallen a little short, Joe thought. "You all were," he interjected. When he turned toward Sandy, he saw tears gathering in her eyes. "Sandy? What's the matter?"

Rather than answer, Sandy pushed open the door with both hands and bolted from the room. Joe started to follow, but Maggie stopped him. "No, let me go after her."

The charm was fading a little from her take-charge attitude. "She's my niece," he reminded her.

"Yes, but I understand her." Maggie left no room for argument. Leaving Joe to stay with Christine and Jennifer, Maggie hurried out of the screening room.

"Uncle Joe, what's the matter with Sandy?" There was frightened concern in Christine's voice.

"I don't know, honey." He wished he did, but he hadn't a clue. It seemed that no matter what their size, women continued to confuse him.

Adam came down the aisle to join them. He saw the look on Joe's face. It mirrored what he'd been feeling lately. "Maggie has a way of taking over."

Joe dragged a hand through his hair. "So I noticed. Was she always like this?"

"Ever since I can remember." Adam found himself in the strange position of defending exactly what annoyed him about Maggie. But she was family and this man wasn't. "Her aggressive manner has its good points."

Joe had observed both sides. "And its bad."

Adam relented and laughed. He and Sullivan understood each other. And from the looks of it, they had something in common. They'd both been plowed under by Maggie. "Yeah."

Maggie quickly caught up to Sandy. The little girl had turned a corner and come to a dead end. She had no idea which way to go next. Confused, upset, she remained where she was, in the corner, her face turned to the wall. Her small shoulders were shaking when Maggie reached her.

Oh, God, she was crying. This was blowing up in her face, Maggie thought.

"Sandy, what is it?" Maggie turned Sandy around and looked at her. The little girl's cheeks were shiny with tears.

Her heart aching, Maggie bent down to take Sandy into her arms. But the comfort she offered was refused. Sandy bore the hug stiffly.

What was wrong? Why was she crying? Christine hadn't even teased her.

"What is it, honey?" she repeated. "Didn't you like what you saw?"

Sandy rubbed away the tears with the heel of her hand. Fresh ones came in their wake. "Yes."

Those were definitely *not* tears of joy. "Then why aren't you happy?"

Sandy shook her head, miserable beyond words and confused about the feelings that she was having. "I *am* happy. That's the problem."

A kernel of suspicion began to form in Maggie's mind. But she didn't want to put words into Sandy's mouth. "Why? Why is being happy a problem, honey?"

Sandy buried her face in Maggie's shoulder. Her words mingled with her tears, both muffled against Maggie. "Because I shouldn't be. It's not right to feel happy when—when—"

Maggie stroked the girl's hair. She'd been right, she thought sadly. "When what, honey?"

"When my mommy and daddy are gone." Sandy began to sob loudly, as if her little heart was breaking. Maggie had a feeling that Sandy had kept everything inside her until this moment. And now the dam had broken, unable to hold things back any longer.

She knew how that was, Maggie thought.

Maggie waited a few moments, letting the worst of it pass. Still holding Sandy against her, Maggie said softly, "They would have wanted you to be happy."

It didn't seem right to be happy when your parents were dead, Sandy thought. But she knew Maggie wouldn't lie to her. Sandy raised her head, blinking tears from her lashes. "They would have?"

"Of course they would have." Maggie rose and smiled down at Sandy. She continued to hold her arm around the girl's shoulders. "They loved you, didn't they?"

Sandy choked back another sob. "Yes, they did." And she missed them something awful.

"You know," Maggie said, trying to keep her tone light, though she felt her own tears rising, "you're a very lucky little girl."

Sandy didn't understand how Maggie could think she was lucky. She was an orphan. She knew what that word meant. One of the kids had called her that at school, saying she wasn't as good as everyone else. "I am?"

"Yes. You had a really wonderful mother and father who loved you and your sisters a great deal. Not everyone does."

Sandy was very quiet for a moment, looking up at Maggie with large, wise blue eyes. It was as if Sandy knew what Maggie meant without really understanding the actual words. "Didn't you?"

A bitter smile threatened to twist her lips, but Maggie repressed it. Instead, she merely shook her head. "No. No, I didn't. And neither did my brothers."

That seemed hard for Sandy to understand. She thought all parents loved their children. Something was wrong. "Didn't you love them?"

"Yes, I loved them." Maggie blew out a breath. She had gone on loving her parents even while she resented the fact that they didn't seem to care about their children, about her. She had never given up hope, until the very end, that something would happen to change everything. To blow away the bad feelings. Nothing ever did.

"And in a way, I supposed they loved me." She rubbed Sandy's cheek. "But they had a lot of problems of their own—"

"Big problems?" Sandy asked. That seemed to be the only reason she could think of why someone wouldn't love Maggie. She knew she did.

"Very big problems." Problems so large they couldn't begin to see how to surmount them, so they never even tried. "The problems kind of got in the way of their remembering that they had other people depending on them." Maggie struggled to scrape the bitterness from her voice. Her parents were long dead. Her hurt should have been buried with them.

But it wasn't.

"My mom died when I was a little older than you," she told Sandy.

Sandy linked her fingers with Maggie's and gave her hand a comforting squeeze. It touched Maggie beyond words. "And your daddy?" she whispered softly.

What a wonderful little girl she was, Maggie thought. She really seemed to care. "He kind of died a long time before that."

Sandy's brow puckered up as she tried to understand. "Kind of?"

Maggie hadn't meant to phrase it like that. The words had just slipped out that way. "It's a long story." She tucked her arm around Sandy's shoulders again. "Maybe I'll tell it to you someday when you're older. For now, I just want you to know how lucky you are to have an Uncle Joe who worries about you and your sisters and wants to take care of you."

Sandy loved her uncle and felt a little ashamed for making Maggie think that she didn't. "I know. He tries real hard." She looked up at Maggie, feeling an instant wave of sympathy, though she didn't know the word for it. "Didn't you have an Uncle Joe?"

"No, I didn't." Neither one of her parents had had anyone in their family who wanted to take on the burden of helping a down-and-out man with four children to raise.

"If you didn't have a mommy or a daddy, or an Uncle Joe," Sandy added quickly as a postscript, "who took care of you all?"

"I did." She had meant only to bolster the little girl's spirits and make her feel better. Maggie had had no intentions of walking down old, shadowy paths again. It seemed, she realized, that since Joe Sullivan had entered her life, she had done nothing but walk down those paths, and frequently.

Joe and Adam had to be wondering where they were. "C'mon, the others are probably worried about you."

She ushered Sandy around the corner. In the distance, she saw the door to the screening room closing. Had Sullivan gone looking for them? If he had, he certainly hadn't had far to go. Why hadn't he said anything?

"I was good, wasn't I?" Sandy asked shyly, bringing Maggie's attention back to her. The note of pleasure managed to squeak through in her voice.

This was turning out all right, after all. Maggie laughed, pleased and hugged Sandy to her. "Yes, you were."

There were things she had to do that numbered in the double digits. How she wound up accompanying Joe and the girls home was still something she was rather uncertain of. One moment she was saying goodbye to them at the studio door, the next moment, she was walking out to the parking lot with them, each hand enveloped in a death grip by the two older girls. Joe had been no help at all.

"There's a penalty for kidnapping in this state," Maggie had warned as she allowed herself to be pulled into the car.

"But they're so young and innocent," Joe protested, closing the car door.

She buckled up. "I was talking about you—not so young or innocent."

He raised his hands to absolve himself of any guilt. "They're doing this strictly on their own. Females have a habit of not listening to lowly males, in case you hadn't noticed."

He smirked all the way to the house.

She let it happen, she realized, because she had gotten caught up in the girls' euphoria even when she knew she shouldn't be.

"Mrs. Phelps," Joe called as he opened the front door. "Break out a case of ginger ale. We have celebrities in our midst."

Mrs. Phelps was long on whimsy and humor. She appeared in the living room with a tray of glasses and a bottle of the girls' favorite soda. Joe poured it as if it were champagne.

"We just made a commercial, Mrs. Phelps," Christine told the woman.

"Ms. McGuire just used the girls for her cookie commercial," Joe explained as he handed out the glasses.

"How nice." The woman smiled at Maggie. Maggie could see why the girls took to the woman. She had a warmth that was evident at first sight.

Jennifer drained her glass quickly, her attention riveted to Maggie. "Can we make another 'mercial?"

Maggie took a sip from hers. "Well, perhaps. If this one tests well and has a good reception, we might want to film one or two more."

Sandy's eyes widened at Maggie's speculation and a smile began to spread. "Really?"

She didn't want to raise their hopes unfairly, but she certainly didn't want to rain on what was very obviously a very sunny parade. "There might be a good chance of that happening, yes."

Christine snuggled over beside Maggie on the sofa. "And this time—"

Sandy surprised them all by cutting in. "Don't start nagging her. Maggie makes all the decisions. Don't you, Maggie?"

Maggie could only grin. "Yes, I do." And some of them, she added silently, apparently successfully.

Joe refilled her glass. What he wanted to be doing was pouring champagne into her glass, somewhere intimate and romantic. But for now, ginger ale in a house full of women, miniature and otherwise, would have to do. "Congratulations, doctor. It seems that the operation was a success."

Maggie raised her eyes to his. She wasn't quite sure what he was driving at. "Excuse me?"

Maybe he could arrange a little time alone with her. He looked toward the girls' nanny. "Mrs. Phelps, would you mind taking the girls into the family room for a while?"

Like a border collie rounding up its charges, Mrs. Phelps began to usher the girls from the room. "Of course not, sir. Girls?"

Sandy, Christine and Jennifer looked disappointed, but for once, none of the girls vocalized a protest as they left Maggie and Joe alone.

Joe turned toward Maggie and sat down beside her. "I mean that you thought doing the commercial would help Sandy feel better about herself and you were right." He raised his near-empty glass to her in a toast, then set it down on the table. "And I'm grateful."

She held the chunky glass between her palms, looking into it. "Grateful enough to forget about asking me any more questions?"

Maggie knew his answer before he gave it.

He laughed softly. "Grateful, not irresponsible." She quirked a brow. "I have a job to do, remember? And we have a bargain."

Maggie sighed. "Yes, we do." She braced herself. She still didn't want to go through with this, but she had given her word. Corny as it might seem to some, her word was something she cherished. At times, it had been the only thing she owned.

There were lines of tension across her forehead. He hated the fact that they were there because of him—more specifically, because she didn't trust him. It bothered him more than he wanted to admit.

"This isn't an execution, Maggie. Just an interview to fill in a few gaps, to confirm a few observations. I've pieced a lot of things together about you myself." She looked at him in surprise, but said nothing. "For instance, I know that your family background isn't that all-American apple-pie picture you've attempted to project."

She wanted to tell him that he was hallucinating, but she knew it was useless. One look at his face told her that. Besides, she'd never been very good at lying. "You were listening this afternoon, weren't you. When I was talking to Sandy?"

Unable just to hang back and wait, he'd gone out looking for her and his niece. When he heard Maggie talking, he hadn't wanted to interrupt.

"Yes."

She felt betrayed, angry. Embarrassed at letting her feelings show. "That wasn't meant for you to hear." She rose, pacing, moving away from him.

There wasn't any place for her to go. It was like the old days, when she'd felt confined, not by the tiny trailer they lived in, but by her very life.

She swung around, her eyes accusing. "I've never told anyone else about that."

He crossed to her and took her hand. "Tell me."

She yanked her hand away. "Why? So you can print it in your magazine and sell a few more copies?" She didn't want to be someone's entertainment over coffee. She'd had enough ridicule at her expense in her earlier years to last a lifetime. It had branded her and made her leery of sharing anything private, including herself.

He thought she knew him better than that. Maybe he was going too fast for both of them. "No, so you can be rid of this dark secret you think you're carrying around."

She didn't like his attitude or his inference. "I don't *think*—"

He bracketed her shoulders and held firm when she tried to pull away. She was so proud, so damn stubborn. "Do you think that you're the first person to ever be poor? Or to struggle to get where she is? There's no shame in that, Maggie."

He could talk. He with his comfortable, loving family, with his supportive parents. He had no idea what it was like to feel orphaned years before the fact. Or to have parents other kids laughed about.

Anger rose in her eyes. "What would you know about it?"

He hadn't meant to raise his voice. Maggie seemed to be able to stir a passion within him that no one else had ever managed to do. He blew out a breath and then smiled. Apologetically, he hoped.

"Not enough, apparently. Tell me about it, Maggie." He took her hand and coaxed her back to the sofa. "Tell me what makes you wake up in a cold sweat in the middle of the night."

"Magazine writers who won't give up." She frowned, but she let herself be led to the sofa. When she sat down again, she found that she just couldn't force herself to relax. "All right, all right, I gave you my word, so here is the story you want so desperately. My father was a born defeatist. He had job after nondescript job and couldn't hang on to one of them."

She knotted her hands in her lap and stared at them. She couldn't face looking at Joe.

"I don't think he ever really tried. Whenever he lost one, it was always someone else's fault, never his. He never blamed himself." Her mouth curved, but there was no humor in the expression. "My mother took care of that for him." She sighed, saying aloud what had plagued her mind for years. "I have no idea why these two people married. Maybe they loved each other once, but I never saw any evidence of it. I never saw them kiss, never heard a good word pass between them."

Maggie took a deep breath as she looked off. "My mother turned to despair, and a bottle, very early in the marriage. Neither one of them should have had children, let alone four." She tried to keep the emotion from her voice, from her soul, but she was past that. "I spent my childhood moving from one trailer park to another. I don't think I owned anything that was new until I was eighteen. It was always someone else's castoffs."

She had to bite her lips to keep the tears from coming, the tears that always seemed to come whenever she thought of the past.

"I swore to myself that given half a chance, I would never be like either one of them. And that my brothers wouldn't have to suffer because of our parents' lack of 'parental concern.'" She felt the pain even through her own sarcasm.

He wanted to comfort her, to hold her, but he knew she wouldn't allow it. "So you became mother and father to them."

She didn't want to sound sanctimonious. "I suppose so."

Sympathy for the girl she had been, the girl who had had her childhood ripped away from her, won out over diplomatic restraint. He slipped his hand over hers. "I don't imagine it was easy."

She laughed softly to herself, looking up toward the ceiling, hoping the tears would remain held in place.

"No, it wasn't. But I managed." Her voice lowered and she was no longer talking to him. She was remembering. "Sometimes, I held on so tight, I thought my fingers would break off." She looked at him, for a moment wanting him to understand her the way she had been. The way she was now. "When you hold on that tightly, sometimes it's hard to let go."

He knew she was talking about her brothers. And the company.

"But you have to," he pointed out quietly. "Otherwise, you can crush the very thing that you've cared for so intently."

He was right, but she didn't want to admit it. "Maybe."

He knew this was hard for her, but it shouldn't have been. She'd made it more difficult for herself than was necessary. "Why wouldn't you tell me any of this earlier?"

He had to ask? Restless, Maggie rose to her feet. "What? That my father was shiftless and my mother was an alcoholic who drank herself to death?" Couldn't he see how she dreaded having that in her past? How it tainted everything? People liked fairy tales; they didn't like reality when it was unhappy. "Would you buy a cookie from a woman with a background like that?"

"Yes." He crossed to her and turned her around to face him. "Because she rose above it."

That was what Ethan had said to her. But she wasn't convinced. "My background isn't something I'm proud of, Sullivan. Above all, I don't tell people about it because I don't want to see pity in their eyes, the way I see in yours right now."

She struggled to pull away, but he wasn't about to let her. Not yet. "And here I thought you were intuitive."

She didn't know what he was talking about. "What?"

He held her closer. "That's not pity, McGuire, that's admiration." He could smell her shampoo, the soap she used, all around him. It was more intoxicating than any Parisian perfume. As was she. "Mixed with a healthy dose of desire."

She wouldn't let herself believe him. Life had taught her to believe in very little outside herself. "There isn't anything more to tell you, Sullivan. You don't have to come on to me." In her mind, she would always be that emotionally abandoned little girl in secondhand clothing. Someone no one wanted. Why would a man as good-looking as Joe want to be with her if it weren't for the article?

He shook his head. It would be funny if it wasn't so frustrating. "You don't get it yet, do you? McGuire, I don't *have* to do anything. Do you think I've been hanging around you just for a story?"

She stared at him, very aware that their bodies were too close for comfort. And that she didn't want to break away even when she knew she should. "Haven't you?"

Rather than answer, he kissed her throat softly and heard her sigh. "Give me a little credit. I'm not a novice. There are ways to get information other than directly from your very tempting lips."

She was having trouble thinking. He was unraveling her as if she were a skein of wool batted around by a kitten. "It would be hearsay," she said with effort, "and I already told you, I've never shared this with anyone."

"Doesn't mean that one of your brothers hasn't." He stopped to look at her. "The skeletons you think you're hiding in your closet might have been out, dancing on the lawn all this time." His eyes held hers. "I didn't need you to make a full confession."

It didn't make any sense to her. "Then why have you been turning up in my classes?"

"I prefer getting my story firsthand, but that's not the real reason." He pressed a kiss to the pulse in her throat and felt it jump. She tasted of all things dark and exciting. "I wanted to be around you."

"Why?" The word was breathy. Maggie felt as if she were sinking, as if her knees were buckling, even though she remained where she was.

"Maggie, if you haven't figured that one out yet, you're not the brilliant woman I've been making notes about for the last few weeks." He took her face between his hands. "Here, tell you what. I'll give you another hint."

Joe lowered his mouth to hers and made the symphony she had heard the last time return, bass drum, cymbals and all.

Chapter Ten

Joe felt his blood racing like a car revving up for the Indianapolis 500 the moment his lips touched hers.

This was the woman who mattered.

The thought throbbed in his mind through the hot haziness surrounding him. What had begun as a physical attraction had quickly escalated into something far greater, far deeper. She was the type of woman he admired. Independent, kind, giving and terrific with the girls. And inside, though she tried to mask it, he knew there was someone who needed a hand to hold. He wanted it to be his.

Desires overtook him and made demands, demands that he couldn't ignore indefinitely. Demands he could just barely keep in check even now.

Reluctantly, Joe stopped kissing Maggie. If he didn't, there would be hell to pay. Feeling like an aroused adolescent, newly thrown into the tumultuous world of emotions, Joe took a moment to catch his breath.

"You know," he murmured, his forehead touching hers, "Mrs. Phelps can be persuaded to stay the night." His mouth curved. "Can you?"

Maggie waited before answering. She felt as if she'd just ended a twelve mile jog. Damn the man. Every time he kissed her, it was as if all the life forces were being sucked away from her. As if she had no will of her own. Kissing him was exhilarating and wonderful and frightening as all hell. She had vowed, ever since she was a child, to be in control of her own destiny, to never fall under anyone else's domination. And here she was, with a man who turned that resolve into wet papier-mâché.

She looked up at him, her insides still the consistency of warmed butter. He was asking her to sleep with him.

Maggie banked down the response that instantly leapt to her lips. She couldn't. Much as her body begged her to, she couldn't. There were just too many complications.

And she was afraid.

Hiding her feelings, Maggie attempted to sound indignant and succeeded only marginally. "Here?"

Did she think he was that careless? He was fully aware of the responsibilities on his shoulders. Just because she was standing there, arousing him the way no other woman ever had just by breathing, didn't mean that he would just throw caution to the wind.

"Actually, I was thinking of your place. I wouldn't want the girls wandering in on us and they do have a habit of bounding in unexpectedly." Especially on the mornings he wanted to sleep in. "They think that my bed doubles as a trampoline."

She drew a deep breath. Her lungs felt constricted, as if she would never get enough air back into them. Even her skin tingled. What was he doing to her?

It took everything she had to form the single word. "No."

He smiled at her, threading his fingers through her hair and combing it back. He saw the hesitation in her eyes.

Mingled with desire. What was stopping her? "Maggie, you don't mean that."

Her mouth felt dry and she was struggling to keep her senses about her. They kept scattering, like tiny silver balls engaged in play in a pinball machine.

"Maybe not, but I'm saying it."

He stared at her, then laughed. "Well, you've lost me again."

If only it were that easy. She placed her hands on his chest and wedged some space between them. It did no good. He would have had to have been in a different room not to affect her. A different room in a different city.

"Sullivan, I lied. There was something else to add to that interview—"

Nothing she could possibly tell him would make a difference in the way he felt about her. He was in for the long haul. Smiling, he wondered what she would say if he told her that she was hopelessly adorable when she was serious.

"You're really a man?" he guessed. His eyes swept over her slowly, touching her intimately. Maggie took a step back as if she had felt him. "Medical science has made great strides." He hooked his finger in her belt, drawing her to him. "Good thing I'm so open-minded."

Maggie batted his hands away, frustrated. Fighting him and her own desires. "This isn't funny, Sullivan."

He raised his hands in surrender and then folded them in front of his chest. "Okay, I'm listening. I'm frustrated, but I'm listening."

He was frustrated? The man didn't know the half of it, Maggie thought. Still, that didn't change her bottom line. One she had adhered to for a long time. "I don't want to get involved."

He didn't believe her, but he played along. "In general or with me?"

"In general." She threw up her hands, exasperated. "And with you."

She might actually believe what she was saying, but he knew better. He had kissed her. He had tasted her desire. It was every bit as real as his.

Joe shook his head. "I think it's too late for those sentiments. You, lady, already are involved."

He was right, damn him. But she couldn't allow herself to give in. She'd lose sight of her goals if she did. Her parents had gotten mired in a marriage and it had destroyed them. If they had once loved each other, all traces of that love had vanished in the face of their conflicts. Promises of love never lasted. Only rejection did. And she had had that.

"Sullivan, try to understand this. I have already raised children." She saw him start to say something and held her hand up, as if to physically stop the words. "Granted, they weren't mine in the strictest sense, but I did raise them." She remained firm. "I don't want to go back to that."

Did she really hear what she was saying? "Seems to me that you never left it."

"Excuse me?" What was he talking about? She wasn't raising children anymore. That was a long time in the past.

She looked bewildered, but he thought it was just denial. "You know what I'm talking about. That 'iron hand in the velvet glove' bit that you do so well."

She shook her head, as if the words were bouncing off. "Now you've really lost me."

He laughed to himself. "I'd like to, McGuire, but I can't. You're like a fever in my blood—" He reached for her.

Maggie pulled away. If he touched her, she was afraid her resolve would dissipate. She hated him for the power he seemed to have over her. "Fevers go down."

"Some of them don't." He knew his desire for her would never fade. It wasn't lust that was at play here. He was attracted to the complete, complex woman, not just to legs that wouldn't quit and a mouth made for loving. He wanted all of her, body and soul. "As for what I said, if you were through raising your brothers, you'd let them fly out of the nest instead of surrounding it with crash pads and pillows to break their falls."

She thought she knew what was coming, but pretended not to. He had no right to say this. "You're not making any sense."

But Joe wouldn't let the subject drop. She had to give up one before she could pick up the other. She had to stop living her brothers' lives for them before she could live her own.

"Aren't I? I've watched you with them. Why do you always have to have the last word? Why do you always have to be in control?"

"I don't—" She sighed. This was useless to argue. She wasn't going to win. Besides, maybe there was a germ of truth in what he said. "Is it wrong to be involved with them? They're my family."

He knew she meant well. Very gently, he took her into his arms. "It's wrong when you get in the way of their finding their own path. Making their own decisions." He remembered what she had told him about letting go. She'd been fighting their battles for so long, taking the heat, it was difficult for her to step back. "They're not the little boys you entertained by making cookies in the trailer."

Her mouth fell open. "Who told you that?"

"Ethan."

She might have guessed. He was the most sentimental of her brothers. Maggie frowned, wondering what else he'd said to Joe. "Ethan talks too much."

"Apparently not around you." If he had, Ethan would have told Maggie how he felt. It wasn't that difficult to see. Joe had picked up on some of his frustration during his interview. And Adam had said as much during the taping. "No one stands a chance around you."

She had had just about enough of this. Her brows narrowed as she pushed him away from her. "If I'm so terribly overbearing and domineering, what do you want with me?"

A thousand and one things, Maggie. "I want you to let go
of what you know and risk something. Risk being with me.
And if you want to nurture somebody, the girls could use it,
not your brothers."

Was he asking for her help in taking care of his nieces?
Maggie frowned. "Is that what this is about? The girls?"

"No, it's about us, but they're going to be part of my life
for a long time. Having you there for them would be an
added bonus, like the ribbon on a Christmas present." He
looked at her pointedly. "A very precious Christmas present. I still don't know what the hell I'm doing. They need a
strong, loving hand to guide them. And you, whether you
admit it or not, need someone to guide. See?" He kissed her
lips again softly, gently, savoring the taste. "The best of all
worlds."

"It won't work," she insisted. She moved, but he suddenly had her cornered. Her back was to the wall, and he
was bracketing her on either side with his hands.

"It will if you give it a chance." God, she smelled good.
Like a man's first brush with heaven. "I've always wanted
the best. Besides," he added, humor glinting the corners of
his eyes, "this way I have a lifetime supply of cookies for the
girls."

When he looked like that, she had absolutely no defenses
against him. Maggie felt her lips curving in a smile despite
all her best intentions. "An ulterior motive."

He nuzzled her, inhaling the heady fragrance he discov-
ered in her hair. "Yeah. In case you haven't noticed, I'm
very devious."

She had to concentrate to keep her head from falling back
as hot sensations poured through her. "I've noticed."

God, he wanted her. "So? Your place?" He played with
a strand of her hair, his fingers lightly brushing against her
cheek. "Or a hotel suite for the night?"

She could feel her breath backing up in her lungs again.
But what he was suggesting, what it would ultimately lead

to, was against everything she had planned for herself. "I'm not into casual affairs, Sullivan. You're moving too fast."

"There's nothing casual about this." He grinned at her. "And it's all relative. You're not moving at all."

Maggie swallowed, trying desperately to collect herself. She couldn't let him wear her down. She'd only regret it if he did. "But I will. And it'll be out of the way."

To illustrate, she tried to push past him. He remained steadfast, like a rock that couldn't be surmounted or circumvented. She sighed, frustrated. "Look, can't we just keep this on a friendship basis?"

But Joe shook his head. That would take more willpower than he had. "I don't want to be your friend, McGuire. At least, not only your friend."

She looked away. "Sorry, that's all I've got to offer."

She was lying, to both of them. He raised her chin until their eyes met. "Your opinion."

The determination that had seen her up from a mind-melting poverty surfaced to preserve her. "Yes, my opinion."

Joe saw things in her eyes that he still didn't understand. Things that were going to take time to unravel. But he had time. He had nothing but time, if it meant getting what he wanted. "Used to getting things on your terms, aren't you?"

He made it sound as if she were a spoiled brat. "In the last few years, yes. It makes things simpler."

The label didn't fit. "This isn't simple, Maggie. Not by a long shot." She thought she could just shrug off what he was offering. He saw things differently. "For instance, I've seen you with the girls. You really care about them."

If he thought he had her, he was wrong. "Yes, I do. But not on a full-time basis." She attempted to wrap her feelings up in a neat, antiseptic explanation. "That's why people like being grandparents. So they can enjoy the best parts."

She was trying to sound disinterested. Who did she think she was kidding? "Like cleaning them up after they've been sick, or helping them through difficult times? Those best parts?''

She blew out a breath. "You're twisting things."

He wasn't twisting things—he was trying to make her face her feelings. Her true feelings. He felt a slight edge to his temper. "I'm a journalist, remember? That's my job. At least, that's what you accused me of doing."

She'd been wrong then, but she didn't want to be wrong now. "This isn't getting us anywhere."

He knew the value of retreat over defeat. "No, it's not. So I'll let you run now." He looked at her pointedly. "But you can't run forever."

Was he telling her that he was her destiny? "Wanna bet?"

When she raised her chin like that, he had an urge to clip her one. He suppressed it, channeling the emotion in another direction.

"Yeah." Joe took hold of her shoulders and kissed her hard, his mouth crushing hers, his determination crushing hers. He managed to rattle his own cage a little, as well. Joe released her, his mouth bruised from hers. "I wanna bet."

The one thing she couldn't deny was the physical effect he had on her. But physical attractions faded. She looked at him defiantly. "Just because you can melt me to mush doesn't prove anything."

The anger faded. Joe grinned. She would have made one hell of an opponent. But he wanted her on his side. "Your opinion," he echoed again.

Joe took her hand. When he began to lead her out of the room, Maggie looked at him warily. "Don't be afraid. I'm not dragging you into my lair. I thought maybe you might want to stay for dinner." She started to refuse, but he was already ahead of her. He knew she had no classes to teach. "It isn't a school night."

"I know, but I've got a meeting in the morning to prepare for." She had already spent too much time here, too much time with him and the girls. How could she possibly remain unentangled in their lives when he persisted in drawing her in like this?

Her excuse carried no weight, and he had a feeling that she wanted to be talked out of it. "Maggie, you were born prepared." He tilted his head back and called out, "Maggie's staying for dinner," then confided to her, "Mrs. Phelps is a terrific cook." He saw the uncertain look in Maggie's eyes. "I've decided to raise her pay and make her our housekeeper, as well."

She didn't want details. She wanted to leave. "I'm sure she's a great cook, but—"

There was no room for a "but." The next moment, Maggie found herself surrounded by all three girls, talking at once. She looked at Joe accusingly. "You play dirty."

If she thought she was insulting him, she wasn't. He looked rather pleased with himself. "Yeah, I know. I play to win."

Two could do that. "So do I." She had to raise her voice to be heard.

Then, Maggie McGuire, you've met your match. Joe merely smiled at her as he went to ask Mrs. Phelps to set an extra plate at the table.

All things considered, Maggie didn't expect to see Joe in class on Thursday. After all, he had gotten what he was after. She'd given him his interview. And she had emphatically turned down his invitation to become his bed partner.

Well, maybe not emphatically, but she had turned it down. Men's egos were frail things and she knew she had bruised his. So there was no reason for him to continue pretending that he was interested in what she had to say in class.

Still, when his desk remained empty after everyone else had taken their seat, there was this morose feeling growing in the pit of her stomach that refused to be reasoned away. It grew to enormous proportions by the time she opened her folder and began her lecture.

She felt the way she had waking up on Christmas morning, knowing that there would be no presents, no tree.

The door squeaked as it opened, catching her attention. Suddenly hope coursed through her veins as if she were an expectant schoolgirl, waiting for her first crush to walk in. It annoyed the hell out of her, but she couldn't help herself.

It felt as if her heart had leapt up into her throat. The little piece of anatomic reorganization blocked any rational thought from continuing on its course through her brain. She was left standing wordless in front of a packed classroom.

Joe saw the stunned expression on her face. Had she thought he wasn't coming? Obviously he hadn't driven home his message about his feelings nearly forcefully enough. He flashed her an apologetic smile. "Traffic."

Maggie noted the way the other women looked at Joe as he took his seat. She wasn't the only one who had missed his presence.

Attempting to maintain a professional decorum, she nodded at his excuse. "We'd just about given up on you, Mr. Sullivan. Glad to see you could join us. Maybe now we can proceed."

He merely grinned at her, as if he could see through her distant manner as easily as if it had been spun out of cellophane.

With effort, Maggie turned her attention to the lesson plan she'd drawn up during lunch. There were only two classes to go and she wanted to give the women who sat in her class their money's worth.

But it wasn't easy.

The number of students who crowded around her desk with questions after class was fewer than usual. She answered them as she tried to gather her notes together and deposit the loose papers into her briefcase. As the last one left, the case slipped off her desk. The papers perversely fluttered out, delaying her exit.

Joe joined her on the floor. "Trying for a quick get-away?" His hands mingling with hers, he scooped up the scattered pages and offered them to her.

She accepted them stiffly. "I have no idea what you're talking about. I've just got a lot of work waiting for me at home."

Joe took her hand and drew her up to her feet beside him. He felt the slight tremble and smiled. Annoyed at the smirk, Maggie pulled her hand away. "Don't you ever get tired of working, McGuire?"

Her eyes narrowed. "Don't you ever get tired of asking questions?"

He raised his brows innocently. "No."

She knew he was trying to goad her, so she struck a calm pose. "I guess it's the same for me."

He leaned his hip against the desk, impeding her progress. "Actually, I'm here on a mission."

She should have known better than to think he'd give up so easily. He was here to try to talk her into changing her mind. Maggie was flattered, aroused and worried at the same time. She wasn't certain just how long she could stick to her principles.

She just knew she had to. "Yes, I know."

Funny how at times he could read her like an open book. "No, not that kind of mission." He saw the faint blush rise to her cheeks and found it endearing. "The girls want to know when their commercial is going to air."

Some of the indignation coursing through her veins was siphoned off. She felt a little foolish. He'd probably orchestrated it to get that effect.

"Oh." On familiar territory, she momentarily relaxed. "Actually, that turned out rather well. It's going to be shown Saturday, during 'One Big, Happy Family.'"

It was a popular half-hour sitcom that was a favorite for the under-fifteen set. His nieces had coerced him into watching the show with them in the name of family togetherness. The program was syrupy, but rather cute and completely innocuous. "How did you manage to get it scheduled so fast?"

She had wanted the commercial on as quickly as possible, to gauge Sandy's appeal and marketability. But the accomplishment hadn't been hers.

"I didn't. Adam did. He pulled a few strings." Maggie smiled as pride bloomed within her. "Seems he once went out with the station manager's daughter. She put in a good word with Daddy."

Joe placed a hand over his chest, stunned. "He did this all without you?"

She raised her briefcase as if she was going to swing it at him. She didn't particularly like being the source of his amusement.

"Look, Sullivan—" Joe was laughing. He had the sexiest laugh she had ever heard. Her annoyance subsided. "All right," she relented. "Maybe I deserved that."

He laid an arm around her shoulders. "Actually, you deserve a lot of credit." He liked the fact that she was backing off a little. It gave him hope. "You're just not superhuman, that's all."

She looked at him smugly. "You haven't seen my crime-fighting cape, have you?"

"No, but I'd like to." He ran the back of his hand along the hollow of her cheek. "Say, possibly the morning after?"

She laughed. The man just didn't give up. They had that in common. Except their goals were completely opposite. "Dream on."

"I do." Their eyes met for a moment and she knew that he was serious. And what he dreamed of. She told herself that she wasn't aroused, but she was lying. "Until that time, what say you come over and watch the commercial with us?"

"I—" Maggie felt the ground beneath her turning to sand. Slanted sand. And it was all pouring in his direction.

He saw another excuse in the making. An excuse probably steeped in the truth. "Don't tell me you're working on Saturday night at eight-thirty."

"I'm not?" Saturdays were no different to her than any other day. There were reports to read, new markets to break into, new avenues to consider. There weren't enough hours in the week to do it all.

She was incredible. "You know that line about all work and no play making Jack a dull boy?"

"I'm not a boy."

His eyes, pure mischief, teased her. "Yes, I know. But the adage still applies."

She wasn't certain she knew where he was going with this. "You think of me as dull?"

With the soul of patience, Joe placed his hands on her shoulders, his eyes holding hers. "No, that's just the trouble—I don't." If anything, he thought of her as too exciting. "But I wouldn't want to see it happen."

Very deliberately, Maggie removed first one hand and then the other from her shoulders. "I wouldn't worry about it if I were you."

"But I do." He leaned in closer toward her. "Is it a date? I'll even supply the popcorn."

She didn't want to say yes. She knew she was going to, despite all the complications that reared their heads. "I'll think about it."

He kissed her temple. "You do that. You think real hard." With that, he crossed to the doorway.

He was walking out, she realized. Without her. She should have been relieved, but what she was was surprised. "You're leaving?"

He wasn't quite sure if that was dismay in her eyes. But he could hope. Joe nodded. "I have to. I promised to turn my article in to the magazine by ten tonight." The crew always worked well past midnight just before they went to press.

Her article. He was handing it in without letting her read it first. He was breaking his promise. She felt betrayal slice through her. It was a familiar sensation, one she had never managed to successfully divorce herself from. "I thought you didn't go back on your word."

He held his hand up to stem the flow of words he saw coming. "Can we back up here? What word are we talking about?"

As if he didn't know. "You said I could have final approval." Suddenly, she felt naked, exposed. She thought she could trust him. That he couldn't hurt her more than she thought possible.

Amusement quirked his mouth. "I had no idea you were on the board of Wild West Parks."

"What?"

"My article is about their new theme park opening up in L.A. *Your* article doesn't go in until next week. *After* you look it over." He crossed back to Maggie and kissed her cheek. "I always had a weakness for egg. In case you haven't noticed, it's all over your face."

She swatted him back. He eluded her, then caught her up in his arms, making her laugh.

He kissed her quickly. "You know, I could always be persuaded to stop by your place after I drop off the article."

After a beat, she wiggled out of his hold. But not too quickly. "Too bad I'm not in the persuading game."

"Like hell you're not." He dropped his hands to his sides. "C'mon, McGuire, get your things. I'll walk you to your car."

"I can walk to my own car, Sullivan. I thought you were in a hurry."

"I'll drive faster." He slipped his arm around her shoulders and guided her out the door. "You know, Maggie, you really don't have to fight me on everything."

No, just on the things that count.

But for now, she kept the thought to herself.

Chapter Eleven

Joe casually slipped his arm around Maggie as he walked her to her car. Dinner, as usual, had been a major three-ring affair. Afterward, all three girls had vied for Maggie's attention. She seemed to be able to manage to give of herself without shortchanging anyone. The girls were crazy about her.

That made it unanimous.

A light, unexpected mist had begun to fall softly. He held her closer.

Maggie felt her pulse accelerating. She tried to justify her reaction with an excuse. She just didn't have any experience in this field. Why else would she react like a high school sophomore every time he touched her?

Because when she had been a high school sophomore she'd been too busy working, trying to provide for herself and her brothers. There had never been that idyllic time for her, the way there had been for others, to wander through love's tender pastures. Her one serious relationship had ended in disaster. She had only herself to blame. She'd been naively underequipped.

She wasn't any better equipped now, she thought. And far too busy for a crash course.

Reasoning didn't help. Her stomach was still knotting.

Joe stopped beside the car, wishing that he could convince Maggie to come away with him for the weekend. Mrs. Phelps was perfectly amenable to staying with the girls. He thought it would give Maggie an opportunity to unwind, to trust him. To get to know him better. He knew all he needed to know about her.

But she had countered by producing an agenda of work with a deadline that was at odds with his plans. She did it each time he made the suggestion.

Eventually, he promised himself, she would run out of excuses. Until then, he would enjoy what he had.

"I can't believe the change in Sandy. In a little over a week, she's become a different little girl." He smiled, leaning against the car and resting his hands casually on the swell of Maggie's hips. Waiting for her to come around was driving him crazy. He'd never had to wait for a woman before. He'd always had more than an ample selection at his disposal. None of them counted. They might as well have not even existed. Only Maggie did.

"She doesn't let Christine push her around anymore." He laughed, thinking. "There's a lot more arguing going on, but since it's for a worthy cause, I can put up with it." Drawing her closer, he pressed a kiss softly to her lips. "And to think, I've got you to thank for the extra noise."

She should be going. Instead, she was standing here slowly getting wet, for crying out loud. Didn't she even have enough sense to come in out of the rain?

Not when Joe was in it.

Damn, but she saw problems looming ahead for her. Big ones. She had no time for a husband, much less an instant family. And she had less than no time for rejection. It still haunted her, like long-forgotten ghost stories that emerged in the shadow of night. Nothing could convince her that if she gave her heart again, she wouldn't eventually be rejected.

"You don't have to thank me," she murmured. She felt his hands as they slipped around her waist, his long, artistic fingers dipping languidly along her hips, and tried vainly to ignore them. "Seeing her come out of that shell is payment enough."

"Shell," he echoed with a laugh. "She won't be there again anytime soon." This was the niece he had watched growing up these last seven years. The stubborn, laughing little girl. Not the sad-eyed child who had emerged the last few months. He knew it had to do with her parents' deaths, but he hadn't been able to find a way to bring her around. Until Maggie. "Thanks to you, she wants to be an actress now."

Linking his fingers with hers, he drew her back to the shelter of the eaves. It was misting harder. He didn't want her to go just yet. The girls were finally asleep. The evening for them should just be beginning, not ending.

Maggie watched the driveway grow slick with moisture and wondered why that seemed impossibly romantic to her. *You definitely don't get out enough, McGuire.* "Most little girls do at her age."

He looked at her and tried to imagine what she had been like as a child. Probably a great deal like Sandy. "Did you?"

She shook her head. Without a television set in her home, the thought of becoming an actress had never entered her mind the way it had with other girls.

She sighed, remembering. "I didn't want to be an actress. I just didn't want to be poor. I wanted to do whatever it took not to have people look at me with pity or talk about my family behind our backs." Emotion brimmed in her voice. "Or worse, taunt us to our face."

He could see her then, vividly. An unhappy little girl in ill-fitting clothing. Moved, he tightened his arm around her shoulders, wishing he could take the memory from her.

Absorb it himself so that it never touched her again. "Was it that bad?"

The smile that rose to her lips was without feeling. "Worse, really." She closed her eyes as she sighed. It was something that she would never be completely free of, that specter of fear that haunted the perimeter of her mind.

Maggie turned to look at him. "Sometimes I wake up in the middle of the night, thinking that everything I've accomplished was all just a dream and I'm back in that narrow little bed with the washed-out comforter, listening to cats rattle the garbage cans looking for food." She struggled to shake off her mood. "I used to feel so sorry for those cats."

He kissed the top of her head. It was damp with mist. Droplets clung to her hair like a crown of pearls. "Why?"

"Because there never was anything for them to eat." She shook her head. "We never had enough to go around, much less to throw out so the cats could eat it." Her mouth curved. "If I had a penny for every time I served oatmeal for dinner... Peanut butter sandwiches were a luxury. To this day, I can't stand to look at either one."

He wanted her to talk about something else, something that didn't drag on her soul as much. "How did you wind up making chocolate chip cookies?"

That had been a supreme treat. She'd been so proud of that, to be able to bring a little simple pleasure into her brothers' lives. The sense of satisfaction had been incomparable.

"Not easily. As soon as I was able, I did odd jobs for people." She had gone from neighborhood to neighborhood, knocking on one door after another. Even then, she had refused to accept the word *no*. "I washed their windows, walked their dogs, mowed their lawns. Anything just to earn some money."

That he could readily visualize. While other girls played jump rope and had tea parties with their dolls, she was out hustling business. "I've never met a handygirl before."

The term made her laugh. She'd learned how to do a great many things out of necessity. Mainly survive. "I was very, very handy."

He turned her around so that she faced him. His eyes held hers. His were full of compassion. "I'm sorry, Maggie."

She stiffened slightly, as she always did when she thought she was faced with pity. "About what?"

He cupped her chin and slowly rubbed his thumb along her cheek. He could see that spark of pride igniting. That spark that attempted to hold back the world. Well, it wouldn't hold him back.

"That you had to go through all that."

She shrugged carelessly. "I'm not." She raised her head defensively. "I mean, I would have given anything to have had a loving set of parents and Christmas with all the trimmings." Even over the bridge of time, it was difficult not to sound wistful. "But in a way, this was good. It made me stronger."

He laughed. "No arguing with that."

Her mouth hardened just a little. It was getting increasingly difficult keeping distance between them. He kept melting it as if the walls she had constructed around herself were all just an ice sculpture. "It taught me that if I wanted something done, I had to do it myself. I couldn't depend on anyone else to do it for me."

He knew what she was telling him. But there was room for more than one in her world. "There is such a thing as carrying it too far, though."

And where had she heard that recently? She couldn't help smiling. "Are my brothers paying you to play devil's advocate?"

Standing here like this, it felt as if there was no one else in the world except for the two of them. As if they were just a man and a woman with an eternity to discover each other instead of a businesswoman and a man with three very real responsibilities depending on him.

"No one has to pay me to do that." He'd never get enough of looking at her, he thought, absorbing her silhouette and locking it away in his memory. "I just want you to know that sometimes you can depend on someone else." He could tell by the set of her shoulders that she was shoring up. He laid his hands on them, forcing her to look at him. "Not everyone is going to disappoint you like your parents and that guy in college who played doctor at your expense."

When he looked at her like that, it was hard to remember her own promises to herself. She said them aloud to reinforce them. "No, because I'm never going to let myself be in that position again."

She had enough determination to carry that out. He hoped she had enough sense not to. "You miss out on a great deal that way."

Maggie pressed her lips together. "Better that way than to get hurt." She firmly believed that. She'd had enough rejection in her life. Only a fool wouldn't learn how to avoid it.

His eyes probed into her very soul. "You don't mean that."

She shrugged him off, moving toward her car again. The mist had abated. The air still felt moist. "You know, you keep telling me what I mean and what I don't mean." Annoyance rose in her voice. Annoyance with him, with herself for hanging around. "You haven't got the faintest idea what goes on in my head." She pulled open her car door.

He laid his hand over hers, stopping her. "Yes, I do." It had taken him a while, but he understood now. "I can see you mirrored in Sandy."

Maggie bit her lower lip. She should have never said anything to him. That had been a moment of weakness, prompted by empathy.

"The little girl the world wanted to push around. You wouldn't have identified so readily with Sandy if you hadn't gone through it in some form yourself."

Admitting it made her too vulnerable. And she already knew what happened to people who were vulnerable. They got walked on. "Adam thought I was like Christine," she pointed out.

He could see the evolution as readily as if it was an equation written out on a page. "You overcompensated."

Her eyes narrowed. She didn't like being analyzed. "Did I?"

He knew a fight in the making when he saw one. Joe was quick to try to defuse it. "I can help you balance things out."

She shrugged off his hands, wishing she could shrug off his effect as easily. "I already told you—"

Actions, he had always believed, spoke far louder than words. "You talk too much."

He felt her mouth moving beneath his in a protest that was never vocalized. His tongue skimmed her lips and the words melted into his mouth, silently disappearing as she responded to him.

The kiss deepened. Whether he was instrumental in doing it or she was, Joe wasn't sure. He only knew that it deepened and that he was falling headlong into the chasm he had created.

His arms tightened around her body, pressing her to him, drawing in the heat, the desire he felt. Like an echo that ricocheted back and forth over the cavern walls, desire fed on desire, passion created passion and reverberated it back.

He had a way of sucking away her thoughts, her will. He made her forget who and what she was. And why. He was taking away her identity and substituting his own in its place.

Maggie pulled away, her chest heaving. She attempted to replenish her air supply and found that her lungs didn't seem capable of holding it. "You have got to stop doing that."

Her eyes were dazed and her mouth mussed with the imprint of his. He liked that, he thought. Liked it a lot. He cupped her cheek, unwilling to break contact just yet. "Why?"

Maggie swallowed, wondering how long it would take for the ground to level out and her equilibrium to return. "Because I like it too much."

He smiled at her. When was she going to get it into her head that resistance was futile? For both of them. "And that's bad?"

She tried not to sound breathless. "Yes."

"Why is that?"

He thought it was a joke, she thought, but it wasn't. Not to her. She wedged her hands between them as he leaned to kiss her again. "Because this isn't what I want. Everything is mapped out in my life. And you're not part of the legend."

The excuse wasn't good enough. "Maps get altered. New streets get built, new roads get put in. Happens all the time, McGuire." He wanted to hold her, but knew that now wasn't the time. She looked too vulnerable and would only hate him if he took advantage of that small opening. Being noble was wearing the hell out of him. "If it didn't, mapmakers would go out of business."

· She saw desire in his eyes and backed away from it. Away from the twin emotions that swirled within her. She had to think with her head, not with the rest of her.

"I don't want a new map. I like the one I have." She was almost shouting. Even to her own ear it sounded as if she was protesting too much. "I like the life I have," she added more softly.

He wondered if she was actually succeeding in fooling herself. She certainly hadn't managed to fool him. "It's a little lonely, don't you think?"

And who was he, the great white knight, riding to the rescue? "Do I look lonely?"

There was no smile on Joe's face as he answered. "Yes."

Defenses flew to the ramparts, armed. "Is that what you're going to put into your article?" A cold fist formed in her stomach. She was always trying to outrun the past, to bury it in an unmarked grave, and here she had told everything. What was wrong with her? "That I'm some lonely, deprived woman who tries to fill the emptiness in her life by working?"

The accusation was as sharp as the blade of a newly honed razor. "I would have thought that after all this time, you would have known me better than that." He tried to temper the pain her words had inflicted. Maggie had known a great deal of adversity and it had made her suspicious of everything. And everyone. "I've no intentions of putting that into the article. Speaking of which, I'll drop it off at your office tomorrow."

Maggie looked at him, surprised. "It's finished?"

He was glad it was over. She couldn't accuse him of ulterior motives now that it was no longer between them. "Yes."

And after he showed it to her, he'd talk to her again about the weekend. He had a friend who had given him unrestricted use of his cabin in Big Bear. Joe could picture Maggie there, by the stream, dressed in only a smile.

She wanted to read Joe's article, but there were two reports she had to review for the upcoming production meeting. "That doesn't give me much time."

Just how carefully did she think she had to scrutinize the material? "I figure you're already familiar with the pertinent points. You're just checking for grammar and spelling."

She looked at him pointedly. "And truth."

Did she think he was going to make things up? "I didn't need to fabricate anything."

No, that was just the trouble. She had given him far too much material. "That's not what I meant. I meant checking for just how much 'truth' you included in the article."

His first impression of her had been that she was utterly self-confident. Was she really so skittish of public opinion? The imprint of her childhood must have gone deep.

"Enough to make it interesting," he said easily, hoping to set her mind at rest, "not enough to make you angry." He really wished that she would trust him. Maybe in time.

He kissed her cheek. "Go, before I change my mind and drag you to my lair."

It was getting late and she should have left half an hour ago. She smiled at the image he created. "The girls would stop you."

He shook his head. "The girls are asleep, remember?"

For a moment, because she was retreating, it was safe to allow other feelings to surface. Her mouth curved. "Don't tempt me."

He liked the sound of that. "Do I, McGuire? Do I tempt you?"

When was she going to learn to keep her mouth shut? He seemed to drag things out of her that she had no intentions of allowing into the light of day. "It's getting late." Opening the door to her car, she slid behind the steering wheel and turned on the ignition.

He leaned in. "Someday, you're going to have to give me a straight answer."

"Maybe." But not tonight.

She pulled out of the driveway as quickly as possible. Her hands felt cold, clammy, as they clutched the steering wheel. He was getting too close to her, she thought, frustrated. She was beginning to care too much about him, about his nieces.

Beginning?

Maggie mocked herself as she felt tears starting to form in her eyes. She was way past the beginning and practically at the home stretch. And she knew what that meant.

Setting herself up for the inevitable rejection. Getting hurt. She hadn't allowed herself to care about anyone besides her brothers for years. The one time she had let her guard down and reached for a normal life, it had blown up in her face, reinforcing what she already knew to be true. That if she became involved with someone, she was going to pay the price.

Talk about a slow learner. Even a gerbil could be trained eventually.

What was she doing, all but living over at Sullivan's house when she wasn't working? Sharing dinners with him and his nieces, putting them in her commercials, spilling her innermost feelings and emotions to him when they were alone?

She was setting herself up, that's what.

She should have her head examined.

But it would be over soon enough, she thought, driving toward the main thoroughfare. After tomorrow, that would be it. There would be no more reasons for her to see him. No more commercials. No more article. No more excuses. Especially not to herself.

All morning long, Maggie had felt antsy, like an islander waiting for a volcano to erupt at any moment. When Joe had said he would drop by with the article for her perusal, he'd neglected to specify a time. Maggie anticipated his appearance with every movement of the clock.

Like a cat on a hot tin roof, she thought disparagingly.

When Ada buzzed her, she physically jumped. "That's it, McGuire," she muttered. "Stay calm and collected under fire."

Blowing out a frustrated breath, irritated at her own reaction, she pressed the intercom line. "Yes?"

"Mr. Sullivan here to see you."

Panic iced through her. Suddenly, she didn't want to see him. Didn't want to read the article and see herself through his eyes. Didn't want it to end and knew it would once she read what he had to say.

She dragged a hand through her hair. Why wasn't life ever simple? "Send him in, Ada."

It was nice while it lasted, Joe.

Her heart was racing as she waited for the door to open. Maggie couldn't remember feeling this nervous even the very first time she had tried to convince Hathaway's to carry her cookies for a month on a trial basis.

Then she had been a woman driven, a woman with a mission. A dream. A woman with faith in her product, unwilling to accept defeat.

Now she was just Maggie McGuire, the girl in the secondhand thrift-shop shoes. Afraid of what lay ahead.

She looked almost white, Joe thought as he walked into her office. Was she that worried about the article? Or was there something else wrong? Something else he was going to have to pull out of her before she shared it with him?

"Well, here it is." He dropped the freshly printed pages on her desk.

With fingers that felt oddly stiff, Maggie picked up the pages.

Was it his imagination, or were her hands trembling ever so slightly? At times, despite what she had told him, Joe still had difficulty reconciling the dynamic businesswoman with the girl she had exposed to him.

She was settling back in her chair, like a prisoner reading charges brought against her.

"You're going to read it now?"

"Yes." She glanced toward him. Her throat felt dry. "If I put it off, I might not get to it."

"That wouldn't be the worst thing in the world." Uneasy anticipation hummed through his veins. He felt like a college freshman again, waiting for the campus newspaper's editor's opinion as he sat in his cubbyhole of an office. Joe gestured toward the sofa. "Okay, I'll hang around in case you want me to strike anything."

She pressed her lips together. *Yes, the whole article.* "Fair enough."

Joe sat down. He could almost hear the air moving around the room as he watched her face while she read. Different emotions passed over her face like migrating storm fronts.

She didn't like it, he thought.

Confirmation was not long in coming. Maggie dropped the pages on her desk. Some broke rank and spread out like the bracing legs of a spider falling to the ground. Maggie raised her eyes. They met across the length of the small room. "You put it in?"

"It" could refer to a great many things. He rose, a soldier defending his boundaries, and crossed to her. Joe looked down over her shoulder, as if the offending item would leap out at him. Or at least glow in blazing red. "What?"

"Everything." She wasn't sure what she had expected. But seeing her life on a black-and-white page had made it seems so stark. So ugly. "The poverty, the dysfunctional parents." She rose, her emotions churning up to a fever pitch she wasn't certain how to control or channel. "Damn it, you even stuck in the part about the thrift-shop clothes."

He wanted to take hold of her shoulders before she really worked herself up. Instead, he stuck his hands in his pockets, knowing that she would take any contact as some sort of compromise. "It's the great American success story. People eat that up."

She wanted distance between them. Distance while she tried to work through this feeling of inadequacy. Somehow, she had thought that at the last moment, he would go back to the plain piece she had envisioned. The one that concentrated on her work, not her past.

"The only thing I want people to eat up are my cookies, not my life."

She was overreacting. There was no reason for this degree of distress. There had been nothing but admiration for her in the article. Didn't she see that?

"What are you afraid of, Maggie? Proving you're human like everyone else?"

He was making fun of her. "I've done the human bit, thank you very much. All I want people to think of when they buy a bag of Magnificent Cookies is that it's a hell of a cookie, not that the woman who built the company wore secondhand underwear until she was in high school."

Why was she so hung up on image? "You could have had brand-new underwear." He gave up the struggle to keep his voice down. "Instead, you spent the money on your brothers, making things better for them. That's pretty terrific."

He didn't know what it was like to be ridiculed. People didn't see the good; they zeroed in on the misery. "I don't care what you think. I'm a private person."

It went beyond that and they both knew it. "There's a difference between being private and being fanatical about keeping everything a secret."

So now he was accusing her of being a fanatic? Maggie drew herself up. "I think you'd better go."

He moved, but it was toward her, not the door. He bracketed her with his hands, as if that could somehow make her comprehend the words. "You think I can't see through this? You're doing this on purpose."

"What are you talking about?"

His eyes pinned her in place far more securely than his hands did. Pinned her in place and made her squirm inwardly. "This isn't about the article letting some woman in Ventura know that you grew up in a series of dilapidated trailers. This is about you and me."

She jerked away angrily. "I didn't see that in the article."

"Then open your eyes." He waved at the scattered pages on her desk. "That was written by a man who's falling in love with you, and that scares you to death, doesn't it? I don't know why, but it does."

She refused to acknowledge his accusation with a defense. Maggie pressed her lips together stubbornly. "I can't give my okay to this."

The hell with the article. "To the article or to us?" His voice was low, dangerous.

Like a shell-shocked warrior who'd forgotten the reasons for the war, only that winning mattered, Maggie dug in. "Both. There is no us, Sullivan. I told you that from the very beginning."

He refused to believe she meant what she was saying. "You said a lot of things. It was up to me as a writer to sort it all out. What I saw was a woman who overcame a great many obstacles to hand her brothers a dream she had for all of them. A woman who said one thing and did another."

Maggie turned away from him, but he caught her by her wrist and forced her to turn around. "Who said she didn't want to raise another family, then got herself involved in mine."

Fisting her hands, she yanked them away from his grasp. "I wasn't involved with you any more than I am with anyone I come in contact with." Frightened, her back to the wall, she heard words coming out of her mouth, hurtful words. "Than any of the people who work for me."

His eyes narrowed. "Kiss them until their socks burn off, too, do you?"

Anger flashed in her eyes. "I've got a meeting to go to."

There would always be a meeting for her. Joe picked up the pages from her desk. There was no reasoning with Maggie now. Perhaps not ever. She had to work this through herself before he could make any headway with her. If he remained, things would be said that neither one of them would be able to take back. They needed a cooling-off period.

He could wait her out. And when her demons threatened to overtake her, he'd be there to fight them off for her.

But not just now. She had to take that first step toward him herself. Everything else would be meaningless unless that happened.

"Go ahead, McGuire," he said quietly. "Go to your meeting. I'll still be around when you run out of meetings to flee to."

Why? Why was he doing this to her? Why was he trying to get her to dissolve her defenses? He'd only leave like everyone else. It was better to leave than be left. "I wouldn't hold my breath if I were you."

"Well, you're not me. And until you stop hiding, you won't have any idea what goes into making up a guy like me."

She felt as if she were attempting to hang on to the side of a mountain with just her fingertips. "I am not hiding." Her voice rose insistently.

He was at the door, but turned and strode back to her. Pulling her to him, he kissed her quickly, soundly, then released her. A promise lingered in the air.

He smiled at her, though it didn't reach his eyes. There, only sadness dwelled.

"Your opinion," he said, leaving.

He heard the thud against the door a moment after he closed it behind him. Judging from the sound, he guessed that it was the paperweight she kept on her desk.

He rolled up the pages in his hand and saluted Ada as he walked by.

Ada continued typing. She knew better than to walk in on Maggie now.

Chapter Twelve

Ethan walked into Maggie's office, feeling a little like Daniel entering the lion's den of his own free will. It helped to remind himself that Daniel had survived the venture.

For the last two weeks, Maggie had been as restless as the liquid within a continuously churning blender. He'd never seen her so unsettled, so unfocused. It was as if something very important had been taken away from her, a corner of her foundation. She was listing and vainly attempting to compensate for it.

And he knew what was the matter. Which was why he tossed the latest copy of *County Magazine* on her desk.

Maggie started as the publication fell on top of the sales chart she was studying. She looked up at Ethan accusingly.

He merely smiled. "Thought you might want to see the article Sullivan did on you."

She pushed it aside as if it were unwanted packing within a box. "I'm not interested."

Ethan sat down on the corner of her desk. He might be playing with fire, but he was unwilling to let the matter go. "Mag-pie, how long have we been together?"

Her eyes narrowed as he knew they would. "That's a stupid question, and you know how much I hate that nickname."

When she glanced down at the chart again, Ethan moved it aside. It earned him a glare. "Yes, I do. I did it to get your attention. You've been moving around like a woman in a daze for the last two weeks."

She didn't like having her behavior questioned, even when it was out of sync. Maggie gestured toward the pile of folders on her desk. "I've been preoccupied."

"Yes, I know."

His attitude irritated her beyond words. Lately, her temper had no fuse. It just flared at will.

"With work," she said between clenched teeth.

Ethan shook his head in solemn amazement. "Two lies in less than two minutes. Must be a record, considering you've never lied to me before." A smile curved the corners of his mouth. "At least, not that I know of."

She knew where this was going. Ethan had an infuriatingly one-track mind, and he'd already shown his preference for Joe. She looked back at the paper on her desk, though there might have been a map of Tahiti in its place for all the sense it was making to her. Nothing seemed to make any sense anymore.

"Wrong. I told you there was a Santa Claus."

For just a moment, he allowed himself to be diverted, remembering. Maggie had tried awfully hard to make life bearable for them back then.

"We always knew it was you." Their eyes met for a moment. His were kind, understanding. He'd come every step of the way with her and although her demons weren't his, that was due mainly to her. She'd kept him and his brothers all safe, all secure. It was time she felt a piece of that warm security herself. "Why don't you stop pretending that you don't miss him?"

Maggie debating denying Ethan's assumption, but he was right. She'd never really lied to him. She couldn't. "Is it that obvious?"

Ethan laid a comforting hand over hers. "To anyone with eyes."

She sighed as she leaned back in her chair. "I can't get involved with Sullivan."

Ethan couldn't understand why she was resisting. He knew Sullivan cared about Maggie. And she obviously cared about the man and the little girls that were in the equation. The entire situation had "Maggie" written all over it. "Not that I don't believe you already aren't, but why?"

It was far too difficult to put into simple words. She shrugged and gestured vaguely around. "Because there's too much work to do."

As far as excuses went, on a scale of one to ten, that didn't even make the scale. "You could always juggle better than anyone I knew. Not the reason." He crossed his arms before his chest. "Next?"

Maggie pushed herself away from her desk and rose. She began to pace around restlessly, the way she'd been doing in her soul these last few weeks. "I don't want to take on another family. I raised you and Adam and Richie—"

Ethan turned his head to keep her within range. He hated seeing her like this. "And we're grateful for that, but I'd like to think we weren't so awful as to permanently sour you on the experience. Besides, I saw you with those girls. You melted around them like a pat of butter on a hot pancake."

She laughed softly as she looked out the window. Was it her imagination, or was the sky less blue lately? "Colorful."

Ethan shook his head. "Truthful. Reason dismissed. Next?"

She blew out a breath, sinking her fisted hands deep into the pockets of her skirt. "There is no 'next.'"

"I think there is." Ethan crossed to her and studied his sister's face for a moment before he spoke. "You're afraid, aren't you."

He knew her better than anyone. There was no point in lying. "Maybe."

There was no maybe about it. They didn't talk about the subject, didn't touch on it at all, but he knew what haunted her.

"Of being abandoned." Maggie looked at him sharply. "Hey, I shared the same nightmares. But they'll never go away until you have someone who'll turn on the light for you and make the shadows disappear. Trust me, I know."

He was right; she knew he was. And yet, she felt that reaching to take what Joe had offered was risking so much. That next step for her was so huge. "And you think Sullivan is that someone."

He did, but he refrained from saying so just yet. "What I think doesn't count, Mag. What you think does." He looked deep into her eyes. "And I think you think the answer is yes—you're just afraid to go for it." He loved her a great deal, and he refused to let her give up this one chance at real happiness because of the scars from an ugly past.

His sister, actually afraid. "I never thought I'd see the day." Ethan ran his hands along her arms, bolstering her, affection in every syllable. "Mag, just because we were dealt a bum hand as far as parents went, doesn't mean everyone else is going to desert us the first opportunity they have."

He searched her face, trying to see if the words were penetrating. "For my money, Sullivan stuck around when someone else would have left." He tugged at a lock of her hair, the way he used to when they were children. "You're not always the easiest person to get along with."

She couldn't argue with that. But there was a very glaring fact Ethan was missing. "He's gone now."

"Because you made him go." He gestured toward the magazine on her desk. "Read the article, Mag." He'd read it, and seen a great deal between the lines. He hoped she was smart enough to see the same thing. "And then call him."

"I already read it, when he brought the draft to me," she said stubbornly.

Ethan tapped the magazine. "Then read it again. With an open mind."

Ethan didn't understand. She shook her head. "I can't call him."

Whatever reasons she thought she had, they didn't count. Ethan kissed her forehead. "The Maggie I know doesn't have 'can't' in her vocabulary. That's what makes her so special." He nodded at her desk as he walked out. "Read it."

The door closed softly behind him. She waited a couple of beats, debating silently with herself. There were no winners.

Maggie crossed to her desk. Taking a large cleansing breath, she opened the magazine and read.

She wanted to find fault with the article, wanted it to reinforce her feelings. She wanted it to cement the position where she stood.

It didn't.

He'd rewritten parts of it. It was an article laced with warmth and admiration. Clear-eyed now, she felt it in every word she read. Joe had come to know all of her, both the gung-ho career woman and the little girl in the thrift-shop shoes who was the mother of the woman she'd become. It had only been her own shame over her roots that had made her read things into the article previously.

Maggie dropped the magazine on her desk, torn.

The indecision lasted only a moment. Ethan was right. She had to swallow her pride and her insecurities and call Joe. If only to tell him that she'd been wrong. She owed that to him. To both of them.

As Maggie reached for the receiver, the telephone buzzed beneath her hand. Damn, she didn't have time for business now.

"You've got a call on line two." Ada's voice floated over the speaker phone.

Maggie frowned. "Tell them I'll get back to them." Her finger hovered over the monitor button, ready to break the connection. She'd wasted too much time already.

"You sure?" Ada sounded surprised. "It's one of those little invaders—"

Why would *they* be calling her? Maggie stabbed down the button with the blinking light before Ada had a chance to finish.

"Hello? This is Maggie. Sandy?"

"No." The childish voice was breathless as it echoed in her ear. "It's Christine." Something was wrong, Maggie thought. She could hear it. "You've got to come over quick."

Maggie reined in her imagination before it could gallop out of the stall. "Is something wrong with your uncle?"

"No, it's Sandy. She's sick." The words were rushing out. "Real sick."

Maggie heard a catch in Christine's voice. Was she crying? This had to be legitimate. Christine wouldn't concern herself about Sandy unless something was seriously wrong. "Calm down, honey. Everything's going to be all right. Where's your uncle?"

"I don't know. He's out." Christine's voice was small, lost. Maggie knew how helpless it felt to be a child without anyone to turn to. "I don't know when he'll be back. She's real bad, Maggie."

Maggie's mind began to race. "What about Mrs. Phelps?"

There was a pause. "She drank something and we can't wake her up."

The words created an instant horrific flashback. Maggie saw herself in the kitchen, tugging on her mother's arm. Her mother was slumped forward, her face flattened against the table. An empty bottle of whiskey lay beside her.

Tears sprang to Maggie's eyes. She brushed them away. This was no time to dwell on her own past. The girls needed her.

Maggie pulled her purse out of the bottom drawer of her desk, then nudged it closed with her foot. She had to get details.

Maintaining a calm voice, she attempted to get a little more information. "Sandy didn't fall down, did she?"

"No, she's just burning up. And moaning. I'm scared, Maggie. Hurry." The line went dead.

The whole thing could very well be completely out of proportion. She knew how easy it was to become frightened at that age. But what if it *was* serious? She had no choice. She couldn't take the chance.

Maggie hurried out of her office and all but walked into Ethan. He'd hung around to see what she thought of the article. He hadn't expected her to come flying out as if she were fleeing something.

"Hold it." He grabbed her by her shoulders.

Ada glanced up as the door slammed in Maggie's wake. "Who set you on fire?"

"Ada, I've got to be out of the office for a while." Maggie tossed the sentence over her shoulder.

Ethan looked at her. "Maggie, the article wasn't that—"

She shook her head, interrupting him. "It's not the article. Christine called. Something's wrong with Sandy and there doesn't seem to be anyone around to help. I've got to see what's going on."

So much for her protests that she wasn't involved with them, Ethan thought, pleased.

"What about your meeting at three with Mr. Pembroke?" Ada asked.

Maggie felt as if she was going in a dozen directions at once. "I—"

"Don't worry about it. Just go see what's wrong." Ethan waved her on. "I'll handle Pembroke."

Joe had said she was standing in her brothers' way. In her zealous attempt to keep everything flowing smoothly, maybe she had been. She looked at Ethan, grateful for his help. Grateful that she could shift the load a little.

"Yes, I know you will." She owed him more than gratitude, she thought, swinging round. "Sorry I've been such a pill about things."

Ethan understood better than she gave him credit for. He laughed. "You were just being Maggie. We all kind of got used to that." He walked with her to the elevator. "But it's nice to see you delegating things for a change."

She nodded. The elevator yawned open before her. "Maybe I should have done it a long time ago."

"Maybe. But better late than never." He reached in and pressed the down button for her. "Go fix whatever needs fixing."

She hoped she could, she thought as the doors closed.

When they opened again in the small lobby, she saw Joe approaching the elevator. Stunned, she hurried toward him. What was he doing here? Why wasn't he home, taking care of Sandy?

She looked like a hummingbird frozen in mid flight. Joe caught her arm before she had the opportunity to rush past him. It had taken a lot for him to come here after the way she'd acted. After what he had promised himself. He wasn't about to let her run off before he had a chance to talk to her.

"How did you know I was coming?"

His question confused her further. "I didn't."

Maybe the situation wasn't as bad as he thought. But she was definitely hurrying somewhere. "Then why are you running off in such a hurry?"

What was he doing, going out when his niece was ill enough to frighten Christine? "Christine just called. She said Sandy was sick." But even as she said it, she was beginning to suspect that perhaps she'd been set up.

Joe was staring at her as if she had just begun speaking in another language. He took her arm and walked her out the front door. Now that he was here, he wanted to talk to her away from this cookie factory she hid inside of.

"I just left the house. Sandy was fine." He smiled ruefully as he held the glass door open for her. "Which is more than I can say about me."

Once outside, Maggie turned around to face him. "Christine said that Sandy was burning up and that she was scared. She said Mrs. Phelps was sleeping. The way she described it, I thought the woman had passed out." The pieces began to fall together quickly. Especially since he was laughing. "I guess I overreacted." She dragged a hand through her hair. "So this is just a hoax?"

Those little devils. This was what came of letting them stay up and watch sitcoms. "I think they're trying to get us back together. This is a lot like the plot of last week's 'One Big, Happy Family.'"

Maggie let out a breath. "I guess there's no point in my rushing over there."

He slipped his arm around her shoulders. "Oh, I wouldn't say that." She felt soft, wonderful, beside him. "They'd be very disappointed if you didn't put in an appearance." He grinned at her. "Why don't you come over and check the situation out for yourself?"

She'd missed him, missed him terribly. But until this moment, until she looked up into his eyes, she didn't realize the intensity of her need for him.

"What are you doing here?" she asked softly.

He combed the hair away from her face with his fingers. "Selling out my pride. I swore I wouldn't return until you asked me back. I guess I don't have as much willpower as I thought."

She'd haunted his mind night and day. Two weeks had been his limit. He'd waited until the article had been on the stands for a day. Not hearing from her had made him take drastic steps. He'd always been able to walk away from situations, from women before. He wasn't walking anymore.

If he could be honest, so could she. "I was going to call you when Christine called."

"Oh?" A smile was forming within him. "Why?"

He wanted his pound of flesh. She'd give it to him. She owed him that. You owed a lot of things to a person who had possession of your heart.

"I read the article again. Ethan practically forced me." She shrugged helplessly, not knowing exactly how to proceed. "He's on your side."

Joe didn't like the way she had worded that. "I didn't know there were sides to this."

"Yes." But not the way he probably thought she meant. "Inside and outside." Her smile was hesitant. "I think he wants you inside our circle."

What someone else wanted didn't matter to him. "And you?"

The smile ceased to be hesitant. "I very rarely disagree with my brothers."

He'd accept that for now. "Won't admit anything, will you?" he teased, ushering her to his car.

Maggie slid onto the passenger seat. She looked up at him. He already knew, she thought. Words weren't needed. He knew. "Not easily."

Joe nodded as he closed the car door. It wouldn't be long now.

When they entered, the house was quiet, and for a moment, Maggie thought that her initial apprehension was justified. Something was wrong. She exchanged looks with Joe.

He could read her thoughts. "They're resourceful," he assured her. When he had left, the three had been in some sort of a huddle. But they'd all been the picture of health and exuberance. "C'mon, let's see what they have planned for you."

Maggie opened the girls' bedroom door. It was a scene, she thought, worthy of an off-Broadway play. Sandy was in bed—Christine's out of necessity, since her own was the top bunk—and the girls were hovering around her. It occurred to Maggie that she had started something by casting the girls in the commercial.

Triumph flashed across Christine's face when she saw Maggie enter with her uncle.

"You're here," she gushed. "Together." She glanced at her sisters. Grant couldn't have looked more satisfied accepting Lee's sword at Appomattox.

Sandy moaned, her hand lying dramatically across her forehead.

"Is it bad?" Concern was written all over Maggie's face as she sat down on the edge of the bunk bed.

"Uh-huh," Sandy whispered.

Maggie touched her lips gently to the girl's forehead. "Just as I thought."

Sandy's eyes widened uncertainly. "What?"

But Maggie didn't answer. Instead, she shook her head. "I'm afraid there's only one cure for this."

Sandy cast an uncertain eye at Christine. "What is it?"

"Tickling." Maggie spread her fingers around the girl's waist. Sandy giggled, wiggling. Maggie gathered her into her arms. "Sandy, you've got my vote for an Oscar."

Sandy didn't know what Maggie was talking about. She only knew that the warmth of Maggie's arms was wonderful.

Christine stared at Maggie. "Huh?"

"Never mind, I'll explain later. I'm just glad you're all right." She looked at the girls. "I've missed you." Maggie raised her eyes to Joe. "All of you."

Jennifer scrambled onto Maggie's lap and threw her arms around her. "And we missed you. All of us." She looked over her shoulder. "Especially Uncle Joe."

She looked at him for confirmation. "Oh?"

"Yes," Christine piped up. "That's why I called you. He's been so sad since you stopped eating with us. Can you have dinner here again?'' To her young mind, that was the solution.

A smile curved Maggie's mouth. "If I'm invited."

In reply, Joe gently swept Jennifer from her perch and drew Maggie to her feet. "You're invited, all right." Ignoring the girls, he took Maggie into his arms. "To every dinner I'm ever going to have. And every breakfast, as well."

She was afraid to hope. But hope rose insistently, anyway. "Just what are you saying?"

This wasn't coming out the way he had planned it. But then, very little of his life had gone according to plan in the last six months. "That you blew me out of the water when I brought the article for you to read. I was going to wait until you finished reading it, then ask you to marry me. But—"

She heard only one thing. The thing she wanted to. She felt sunshine bursting within her. "Yes."

Joe closed his mouth, then opened it again. "What?"

"I said yes." Maggie wound her arms around his neck. There was no way to describe what she was feeling inside. As if she had finally, after all these years, found a place for herself. "Yes, I'd love to marry you." Just saying the words brought peace and excitement to her at the same time.

He couldn't quite get himself to believe it was true. And he definitely hadn't meant to propose to her in the middle of his nieces' bedroom. "Just like that? After all you've put me through, you've changed your mind? You're not afraid anymore?"

It wasn't that easy. But it was something she could work at. "No, I'm still afraid. But when I was little, I always wanted someone to hold me when I was afraid, to make it all better."

"One set of arms at your disposal." He tightened his hold around her. Her body fit neatly against his. "Yours to use for as long as you want."

She tilted her head back, her eyes on his. "How does forever sound?"

"Doable. Very, very doable." He kissed her forehead, aching to kiss her the way a man kissed a woman he'd sworn his soul to. Soon, he promised himself. Very, very soon. "I won't walk out on you, Maggie. Not even if you push me out. I can't. I love you and I need you too much. I need to feel my blood rush when I kiss you. I need to see you smile." He cupped her cheek gently. God, but he loved her. "The girls are crazy about you and you make a hell of a chocolate chip cookie. I can't find a better one on the market."

She laughed, dizzy with the sensation coursing through her. "There isn't one."

His mouth whispered along hers. "So I've learned." Maggie rose on her toes, ready to sink into the kiss. She felt a tug on her skirt.

"Are you and Uncle Joe getting married?" Christine asked.

"Yes." Maggie grinned at him. Saying it felt incredible. "Yes, we are."

Christine seemed to take it in stride. There was only one thing concerning her. "Can I be the flower girl?"

Sandy immediately positioned herself in front of her sister. "No, pick me."

Christine elbowed Sandy out of the way. "You talked in the commercial. I get to throw the flowers."

Maggie saw a free-for-all in the making. She laughed as she felt Joe's arms tighten around her. "Hold it, you can *all* be my flower girls—as long as you promise not to throw the flowers at one another."

Christine didn't look pleased with the solution at all, though it seemed to sit well with her sisters. She tapped her foot impatiently. "But—"

This could continue for some time. Joe had better things for Maggie's lips to be doing than arguing about the details of the wedding. He turned Maggie's face toward his. "Let them work it out for themselves."

She knew he was right. Right about a lot of things. "Okay."

And then he kissed her before she could come up with another answer.

*   *   *   *   *

COMING NEXT MONTH

#1102 ALWAYS DADDY—Karen Rose Smith
Bundles of Joy—Make Believe Marriage
Jonathan Wescott thought money could buy anything. But lovely
Alicia Fallon, the adoptive mother of his newfound baby daughter,
couldn't be bought. And before he knew it, he was longing for the
right to love not only his little girl, but also her mother!

#1103 COLTRAIN'S PROPOSAL—Diana Palmer
Make Believe Marriage
Coltrain had made some mistakes in life, but loving Louise Blakely
wasn't one of them. So when Louise prepared to leave town, cajoling
her into a fake engagement to help his image *seemed* like a good idea.
But now Coltrain had to convince her that it wasn't his image he cared
for, but Louise herself!

#1104 GREEN CARD WIFE—Anne Peters
Make Believe Marriage—First Comes Marriage
Silka Katarina Olsen gladly agreed to a platonic marriage with
Ted Carstairs—it would allow her to work in the States and gain her
citizenship. But soon Silka found herself with unfamiliar feelings
for Ted that made their convenient arrangement very complicated!

#1105 ALMOST A HUSBAND—Carol Grace
Make Believe Marriage
Carrie Stephens was tired of big-city life with its big problems.
She wanted to escape it, and a hopeless passion for her partner,
Matt Graham. But when Matt posed as her fiancé for her new job,
Carrie doubted if distance would ever make her truly forget how
she loved him....

#1106 DREAM BRIDE—Terri Lindsey
Make Believe Marriage
Gloria Hamilton would only marry a man who cared for *her*, not just
her sophisticated ways. So when Luke Cahill trumpeted about his
qualifications for the perfect bride, Gloria decided to give Luke some
lessons of her own...in love!

#1107 THE GROOM MAKER—Lisa Kaye Laurel
Make Believe Marriage
Rae Browning had lots of dates—they just ended up marrying
someone else! So when sworn bachelor Trent Colton bet that she
couldn't turn him into a groom, Rae knew she had a sure deal. The
problem was, the only person she wanted Trent to marry was herself!

MILLION DOLLAR SWEEPSTAKES (III)

No purchase necessary. To enter, follow the directions published. Method of entry may vary. For eligibility, entries must be received no later than March 31, 1996. No liability is assumed for printing errors, lost, late or misdirected entries. Odds of winning are determined by the number of eligible entries distributed and received. Prizewinners will be determined no later than June 30, 1996.

Sweepstakes open to residents of the U.S. (except Puerto Rico), Canada, Europe and Taiwan who are 18 years of age or older. All applicable laws and regulations apply. Sweepstakes offer void wherever prohibited by law. Values of all prizes are in U.S. currency. This sweepstakes is presented by Torstar Corp., its subsidiaries and affiliates, in conjunction with book, merchandise and/or product offerings. For a copy of the Official Rules send a self-addressed, stamped envelope (WA residents need not affix return postage) to: MILLION DOLLAR SWEEPSTAKES (III) Rules, P.O. Box 4573, Blair, NE 68009, USA.

EXTRA BONUS PRIZE DRAWING

No purchase necessary. The Extra Bonus Prize will be awarded in a random drawing to be conducted no later than 5/30/96 from among all entries received. To qualify, entries must be received by 3/31/96 and comply with published directions. Drawing open to residents of the U.S. (except Puerto Rico), Canada, Europe and Taiwan who are 18 years of age or older. All applicable laws and regulations apply; offer void wherever prohibited by law. Odds of winning are dependent upon number of eligibile entries received. Prize is valued in U.S. currency. The offer is presented by Torstar Corp., its subsidiaries and affiliates in conjunction with book, merchandise and/or product offering. For a copy of the Official Rules governing this sweepstakes, send a self-addressed, stamped envelope (WA residents need not affix return postage) to: Extra Bonus Prize Drawing Rules, P.O. Box 4590, Blair, NE 68009, USA.

SWP-S895

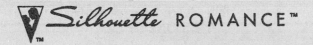

Silhouette ROMANCE™

Silhouette Romance presents the latest of Diana Palmer's much-loved series

Long Tall Texans

COLTRAIN'S PROPOSAL
DIANA PALMER

Louise Blakely was about to leave town when Jebediah Coltrain made a startling proposal—a fake engagement to save his reputation! But soon Louise suspected that the handsome doctor had more on his mind than his image. Could Jeb want Louise for life?

Coming in September from Silhouette Romance. Look for this book in our "Make-Believe Marriage" promotion.

DPLTT

As a $\mathscr{P}$rivileged $\mathscr{W}$oman, you'll be entitled to all these $\mathscr{F}$ree $\mathscr{B}$enefits. And $\mathscr{F}$ree $\mathscr{G}$ifts, too.

To thank you for buying our books, we've designed an exclusive FREE program called *PAGES & PRIVILEGES*™. You can enroll with just one Proof of Purchase, and get the kind of luxuries that, until now, you could only read about.

$\mathscr{B}$IG HOTEL DISCOUNTS

A privileged woman stays in the finest hotels. And so can you—at up to 60% off! Imagine standing in a hotel check-in line and watching as the guest in front of you pays $150 for the same room that's only costing you $60. Your *Pages & Privileges* discounts are good at Sheraton, Marriott, Best Western, Hyatt and thousands of other fine hotels all over the U.S., Canada and Europe.

$\mathscr{F}$REE DISCOUNT TRAVEL SERVICE

A privileged woman is always jetting to romantic places. When <u>you</u> fly, just make one phone call for the lowest published airfare at time of booking—<u>or double the difference back</u>! PLUS— you'll get a $25 voucher to use the first time you book a flight AND <u>5% cash back on every ticket you buy thereafter through the travel service</u>!

SR-PP4A

FREE GIFTS!

A privileged woman is always getting wonderful gifts.
Luxuriate in rich fragrances that will stir your senses (and his). This gift-boxed assortment of fine perfumes includes three popular scents, each in a beautiful designer bottle. <u>Truly Lace</u>...This luxurious fragrance unveils your sensuous side. <u>L'Effleur</u>...discover the romance of the Victorian era with this soft floral. <u>Muguet des bois</u>...a single note floral of singular beauty.

YOURS FREE!

$50 VALUE

FREE INSIDER TIPS LETTER

A privileged woman is always informed. And you'll be, too, with our free letter full of fascinating information and sneak previews of upcoming books.

MORE GREAT GIFTS & BENEFITS TO COME

A privileged woman always has a lot to look forward to. And so will you. You get all these wonderful FREE gifts and benefits now with only one purchase...and there are no additional purchases required. However, each additional retail purchase of Harlequin and Silhouette books brings you a step closer to even more great FREE benefits like half-price movie tickets... and even more FREE gifts.

L'Effleur...This basketful of romance lets you discover L'Effleur from head to toe, heart to home.

Truly Lace...
A basket spun with the sensuous luxuries of Truly Lace, including Dusting Powder in a reusable satin and lace covered box.

Complete the Enrollment Form in the front of this book and mail it with this Proof of Purchase.

PROOF OF PURCHASE
Offer expires October 31, 1996

SR-PP4